Dedicated to my husband, Anthony, for his unconditional love, support and devotion.

A few words from the Author

Answering requests from friends and family to write something a little more edgy, this book is a little different to the previous two and has been an interesting challenge for me, although, one I enjoyed immensely as the storyline began to develop in my mind. I hope that you will also find enjoyment in these pages as you keep turning them.

I would like to take this opportunity to acknowledge my thanks to the very special people who have helped me to create and polish this book; the third in my evolving journey as a writer.

Firstly, to my husband Anthony, for his unwavering support and encouragement. Having been the listener during my read-aloud-phases, Anthony was the first and last one to hear this story; his suggestions greatly appreciated, along with his belief in this being the best book so far!

My thanks also extend to my niece, Samantha and friends, Rachel, Merrenna and Janet, for their valuable help, encouragement and honesty, during the whole review process. It is not always easy to be a reviewer and critic, unless that is your job, but these amazing women stepped up to the plate for me *and* met my critical deadlines willingly.

To the team at New Generation Publishing, my thanks also extend to each of you, for always being at the end of the telephone, whenever there are questions to be asked.

Finally, my undying thanks go to you, my reader, for buying this third book and supporting my journey as a writer. I sincerely hope you enjoy this storyline and if you do, please feel free to share your thoughts via my social media pages, or the online review options from your chosen book-retailer.

Thank you all!

Contents

Chapter 1

Sharing Life Experiences

Happiness and success go hand-in-hand with good food, good service and Teamwork! The sign above the bar in Antoine's Bistro lived up to its meaning and since opening a year ago, the welcoming ambience and relaxed atmosphere had regularly brought customers flocking in, each one wanting to try out the delights of Antoine's culinary expertise. Kate and her friends were no exception, having become regular customers following the big opening night. Which Antoine had hosted with his famed charismatic charm and grace. The group of friends had fallen in love with the French-Caribbean styled bistro and very quickly established a weekly routine of meeting there straight from work. Often, putting the world to rights whilst enjoying the delights of Antoine's menu and wine cellar.

After consuming several glasses of the best rosé, this particular evening found the girls delving into funny secrets involving ex-boyfriends, including, some of the worst and unceremonious ways they had been dumped. Which, unsurprisingly, had led to several gasps and outbursts of raucous laughter. It was Kate's turn to share. "Well, mine was Rob, who said that whilst I was a lovely person, I really needed to be a bit more of a bitch."

"What?" Shelley's giggly mood waned instantly, feeling aghast that anyone would say such a thing, let alone Kate's Rob.

"Why did he want you to be more of a bitch?" Emily's normally beaming smile now replaced by surprised disbelief.

"What does that even mean?" Shelley asked, irritated by and still trying to make sense of Rob's statement. "… And why would he want that kind of girlfriend anyway?"

Inga hadn't actually known Rob, but, sensing a bubbling outburst, she wanted to take the sting out of the conversation. "Maybe, he was looking for a dominatrix?"

It worked, her little interjection caused them all to laugh as Kate continued with her story, "What made it worse was that Rob didn't even have the balls to tell me to my face, he just sent a text and basically dumped me there and then."

"No way!" Kate's three friends' voices shrilled slightly, with a combined reaction of shock, disbelief and anger. Kate felt quite calm talking about it now – even speaking about it in a fairly matter-of-fact kind of way – but there had been a time when that text had reduced her to tears every time she had thought about the *what could have been* scenario. Thankfully, she was past that now.

Inga was still scowling at the idea of Rob even saying such a hurtful thing, "Well, I think he was an idiot to let you go!"

Shelley nodded her blonde-curly head in agreement. "Inga's right Kate, it's his loss and clearly you're better off without him. Besides, you've got the very lovely Pete now."

Shelley winked knowingly at Kate, who nodded and laughed as she replied, "I do indeed."

Sipping on her glass of rosé, Kate realised how cleansing it felt to offload the final dregs of her broken relationship. It had been a secret she'd withheld for far too long.

"To be honest with you girls, that whole situation kick-started me into looking at myself and how I could have done things differently, not just with Rob, but some of the other broken relationships I've had. I was convinced I was the common denominator, so, I started to look at how to fix me, or at least try and understand why relationships never seemed to work out for me beyond a few months." The girls listened intently. "It was an interesting journey, although I'll be honest enough to admit, one that was pretty hard to swallow at times. Mainly because after reading loads of self-improvement books, I realised I'd actually been my own worst enemy all along."

"What do you mean, Kate?" Emily jumped in first. Her bubbly personality perfectly matched her reddish-blonde hair, as she waited for Kate's response, eager to hear any wise words of self-taught wisdom. Inga and Shelley just listened, recognising an all too familiar self-doubt.

"Well, it turns out he was right. About me being too nice I mean. Basically, I'd been trying to help him when he hadn't even asked for my help and I tried to fix things for him, thinking I was making his life easier and nicer." Ironically, Kate could smile about it now.

"What's wrong about that?" Emily asked the question they all wanted to know the answer to.

"Well, Em, men are inherently life's 'fixers' and they need to do stuff for themselves, which also means that if they need our help, they'll ask for it. The clincher is, if they don't ask for our help, we have to butt out and leave them to fix their own problems."

"Huh? How's that?" Inga's mind was inquisitive and eager to pick up tips related to understanding her man better.

"Well, if we interfere, it's like we're taking their power away from them." Saying it out loud now, made it sound so obvious to Kate, that she couldn't believe she hadn't recognised or understood that fact before.

"Whoa, that's deep." Shelley was slightly sceptical of the self-help advice which Kate had picked up from her books.

Emily and Inga admitted that they too had often 'helped' their men without invitation, "It's just the nice thing to do, isn't it?" Emily asked the question which seemed like a no-brainer to her.

Kate understood her reasoning. "Well, that's what I thought too, Em, but apparently, it really bothers some men and makes them feel useless."

"I *still* don't get it, why wouldn't a guy want your help?" Shelley was puzzled and thought that maybe it was the wine messing with her head.

"…and therein lies the problem Shelley, we think differently to men. It's because he's from *Mars* and we're from *Venus*." [A reference to the book *Men are from Mars, Women are from Venus*, by John Gray, and one of the books Kate had learnt so much from.]

As the girls raised their eyebrows, Kate explained that it was true. "We really *are* two very different species and quite honestly, I'm amazed any heterosexual couples manage to live together as well as they do. All I can say is, there are obviously some guys who are clearly more tolerant and flexible than others."

"Thank God for that, or Dave will be moving out real soon!" Shelley retorted, laughing. The others joined in, lightening the mood again. Dave was Shelley's rock, an easy-going casual kind of guy, who was taller than her and a bit on the heavier side, but who was such a good laugh. Dave had a fun way about him and always managed to make Shelley smile, often teasing her about some of the strange people she met through her work as a reporter.

Inga was married to the very handsome and ripped, Damien, who often worked away from home for long periods at a time. It was a dangerous life for a tall, handsome guy, who could pull any woman he wanted. But, with eyes that bewitched him and dainty elfin features, framed by a chic, cropped style of hair, Inga was absolutely beautiful and Damien, who had always felt protective of her, had never wanted to stray. Inga took care of him in every way. Yet she always looked as though any man could prise her away from him, if she so desired that to happen. Something Damien was always very aware of. Spending so much time apart was difficult for them both and a big factor in the sticky patch they were currently going through.

With tensions running a little higher than normal, Inga was keen to pick up some pointers on how they could maybe improve things. "So, what else did the books say about how we should be with our men, Kate?"

"Ah, well, another little gem of advice I found really interesting was, that men really *do* need their cave-time."

"What? You gotta be kidding me? Seriously? Cave-time? Why?" Shelley's voice was lined with sarcasm. "Do they want to be alone?"

Kate grinned at Shelley's Greta Garbo impression attempt and explained what she meant. "Apparently, men need a bit of cave-time when they've finished work, to unwind and do *blokey* things, before they jump back into family life." Kate paused as the girls huffed with indignation. "What I mean is, take Jed for example" – Jed is Emily's boyfriend – "he goes to the gym after work, so he gets his 'alone' time away from Emily. But, that doesn't mean he doesn't love her, he just needs to unwind from work, do some macho *him* stuff, then he's on-point to spend time with Emily, doing whatever she wants him to join in with."

Inga sighed. "Ah, I get it, that does kind of make sense, when you put it that way, although it does also sound a bit selfish of men." Inga felt disappointed at the thought that Damien might want more time away from her.

Shelley wasn't so convinced, "A *bit* selfish?"

"Actually Kate, I think you do have a point there, I mean, whenever Jed doesn't go to the gym straight from work, he does get a bit tense and moody." Emily was now reconsidering Jed's gym-time in a new light and not minding it quite so much.

"So, what about us girls then, Kate? Don't we need our own cave-time too?" Shelley was desperate to balance out this male/female injustice.

"No, we don't, well, not quite in the same way as the guys, but that's because we're built different. I mean we do need our own *me-time*, but it's not the same as the guys. We can cope with bigger gaps between whatever me-time we choose for ourselves. But, being women, we do need our men to listen, without always trying to fix everything for us and just be interested in hearing about what happened during our day..."

"Bahahaha, *interested* and therein lies the challenge." The girls all laughed at Shelley's statement of the obvious.

"I have to say, I always *wish* that Damien would spot things that might need fixing, but more often than not, he doesn't even notice!"

"I know what you mean, Inga, but that's something different again. Women also notice things more than men do. I mean, how many times have you walked into a room, scanned it and spotted something out of place, or broken? Then Damien walks in and just sits down, oblivious to anything that needs attention?"

Inga laughed as she responded, "All the time. You're so right, Kate."

"Anyway, all of that made me realise how I was always 'doing' stuff for Rob and being 'nice'. I just didn't realise at the time, that it would be a problem for him."

"Well, more fool him then, Kate. It's his loss that he's missed out on such a wonderful woman and you mark my words, he'll regret it one day!" Emily was convinced of that fact and felt lucky to have her Jed, who always complimented her and didn't mind that she wasn't necessarily the prettiest or slimmest girl in their group. To Jed, Emily was all woman and he loved her just the way she was, he never wanted nor expected her to change her appearance. Emily was his perfect woman and in fact, Jed made sure *he* worked out and kept trim for *her* as much as himself, knowing his muscular physique turned her on; that was his reward and he loved the fact that he and Emily shared an amazing sex life.

"Thanks, Em. I guess it all helps us to grow as people, eh?" Kate appreciated the loyalty of her friends, but she was fine now and completely over Rob, not only that, she was totally in love with Pete.

Just before meeting Pete and to leave the old Kate behind, she'd decided to freshen up her 'look', which included a new hairstyle and resulted in Kate feeling like a new woman afterwards. Fresh and exciting, with no regrets at having swapped her fabulous long brunette locks in favour of a chic bob. The shorter style really suited Kate and had drawn a compliment from Pete on the very first night they met. Pete had a thing for brunettes and Kate's dark eyes with her long lashes, had drawn him in from the moment he'd said, 'Hello'. Kate herself, had been instantly and physically drawn to the rugged, yet handsome man, who had stolen her heart when she had least expected it. Pete's look had tempted her animalistic instincts and Kate had wanted to know him more intimately from the word go – what was not to like after all – Pete oozed sex-appeal as far as Kate was concerned, he was strong, confident and seemed totally in control of whatever situation got thrown at him.

Inga admired the strength and confidence Kate now had and wished that she too could be more like her. Lately, due to the worry about hers and Damien's relationship, Inga had been feeling less confident, but now feeling more impulsive, she decided it was time for a change. So, when Damien got back from his latest job, they would sit down and talk properly. Inga loved Damien very much and really wanted them to work through their problems together, before anything got so big that they found themselves parting company. It was true that Damien had become a bit distant more recently and this felt like the right time to tackle whatever it was that was wrong between them.

The evening had flown by and Antoine's team had already begun clearing the tables in readiness for their closing-up routine. The girls agreed they'd best get off home and, as was their custom before parting company, they raised their glasses to toast another great evening of good food, friendship and happy times ahead. As their glasses clinked, the girls grinned at each other, grateful for the comfortable friendship they shared.

Chapter 2

A Strange Dream

Kate was nursing a headache when she woke up in the middle of the night. Having drunk far too much wine at Antoine's, she now had a mouth which felt like the Sahara Desert. Carefully reaching for the glass of water on her bedside table, she groaned silently, remembering that her headache pills were in the bathroom cabinet. Reluctantly, she dragged herself out of bed and tiptoed across the room, trying not to wake the sleeping Pete, who was lying next to her. Not that she needed to worry, because by the sound of his snoring, her boyfriend was well and truly in the Land of Nod.

Pete stayed over at Kate's regularly and lately, that had become a habit which had evolved into pretty much every free night that he had. Being an independent helicopter engineer, Pete's skill in servicing and repairing the expensive mechanical birds was in great demand and often took him up and down the country, working for the private sector, as well as various county air ambulance and coastguard rescue teams. The best part of his job was knowing that keeping the birds flying was also saving lives. The worst part was the fact that it took him away from Kate a lot. Otherwise, Pete loved his job and lately, he'd come to realise that he loved Kate too.

Kate had first met Pete at the launch of Antoine's bistro and the two of them had hit it off immediately, talking long into the night as the party happened around them. Several dates had followed quickly after that and it wasn't long before they were considered 'an item' as their regular dating took on a more serious stance. Pete was a lovely guy and he treated Kate like she was the most special person on earth; her friends adored him for that and Kate, well, she loved him, that much was beyond doubt to her friends, and happily, Pete knew it too.

Antoine had recognised that Pete was in love, almost from the first moment he'd met Kate. The two men had been friends since their early school years and had an unbreakable bond of friendship and understanding, which both of them treasured. The two had always worked hard as well, each earning the respect of their peers, whilst being lucky enough to have been successful in their very different career choices. Thankfully, they were both now reaping the benefits of all those labour-intensive years.

On the night of Antoine's launch and having caught sight of Kate from across the room, Pete had been struck by the vitality and enthusiasm she'd exuded, his attention unwavering as he'd watched her entertaining the small group of people standing with her. Feeling intrigued enough to find out more about the woman who had captured his attention, Pete had asked Antoine about her. On seeing how smitten his mate clearly was, Antoine had admitted that, as much as he would like to take the credit, it was pure chance that Kate was even there, being the 'plus one' guest of Dan, a local firefighter who also happened to be Kate's cousin. Relief had washed over Pete's face when he realised that Dan was not 'Mr Kate', and Antoine had watched with twinkling eyes as his best mate, so obviously bitten by the love-bug, couldn't take his eyes off Kate. Encouraging Pete to go and speak to her, Antoine was relieved when he did. One thing he had realised from his earlier introduction by Dan was that Kate was currently single. First impressions had been good and Antoine had immediately warmed to Kate. With the family genes she had, he imagined that like Dan, Kate would be a really nice person. Dan was one of the best and Antoine liked him very much.

When Pete first walked towards the leggy beauty across the room, Antoine noticed the slight lift in his step and smiling to himself, he turned away as Pete casually joined Kate's group. Almost immediately, the people talking to her also happened to turn away to mingle with other guests. Wanting to gain Kate's interest and attention, Pete immediately offered to refill her now empty glass with the complimentary wine being walked around by Antoine's staff. It worked and Kate beamed a dazzling smile at Pete, before adding a gracious, "Thank you," and asking Pete how he knew Antoine. Responding with a few stories from their childhood, Pete totally relaxed as he chatted to Kate, asking her about her life too and enjoying the easy conversation that followed.

As well as being a friend of Kate's, Shelley was also the reporter from their local paper and working the launch, taking photos of guests. On receiving the invited list of names, she was relieved to see that she would know at least two of the guests. Kate's cousin Dan being the other person she knew. As Shelley worked the party she bumped into Dan, who quietly confided in her that Kate seemed to be hitting it off with a guy called Pete. Intrigued, the two of them had watched from a distance, as the intense crackle of chemistry between the pair became evermore apparent. Shelley had grinned at Dan, feeling equally pleased for Kate. Naturally, as her best friend, she was also desperately interested in knowing more about this man, Pete. So, excusing herself from Dan's company, Shelley carefully circulated the room, gathering snippets of information for her report, whilst she casually skirted around Kate and Pete, who were totally oblivious to anyone else in the room. It was obvious to Shelley that the two of them only had eyes for each other, which made her heart lift. Catching Dan's watchful eye, Shelley shared a knowing wink and smile with him.

Since that day, time with Kate was often interrupted by Pete's work. But, those breaks from each other seemed to work well for the two of them and they were very happy spending time together whenever they could, always making the most of every moment. Even when they decided to set up home together, Kate and Pete had seemed to blend easily. Neither one took the other for granted and that important gesture had made all the difference to them both. Along with laughter and great sex, those three important things formed the key to their very contented relationship.

Kate returned to bed, headache pills taken, hoping they would work instantly, which of course, they would not. Pete stirred and asked if she was okay, then whispered something inaudible, as he simultaneously pulled her towards him, then promptly fell asleep again. Lying still, so as not to disturb Pete any further, Kate was trying not to over think the random thoughts that, along with the headache, were now pushing the sleepiness out of her mind; her brain was too wide-awake with thinking about that evening's chatter with the girls. Staring into the darkness and listening to Pete's even breathing, Kate briefly wondered what Rob was up to and if he had met his Miss Right? As the thought entered her head, she decided to believe that all was well with Rob and pushing him out of her mind again, she snuggled up to Pete, very much appreciating what a fabulous and very different guy he was and how much she truly loved her Action Man. It took around twenty minutes for her headache to subside and as Kate eventually drifted off to sleep, she went straight into an intense dream.

It was one of those dreams where everything feels very real, yet, is different to anything or anywhere you already know. In the dream, Kate was feeling happy as she walked along a sunny street lined with cafés and bars, each one welcoming customers as if they were on holiday. It was a street which Kate did not recognise, yet at the same time, she instinctively knew there was a junction just ahead. On one corner was a diner, which opened from early morning to late evening and on the other, a bakery, which also sold the best fresh bread for miles around. Trapped in her dream, as Kate walked past one pavement café, an older lady stepped out in front of her and turning left, caught her handbag on the post that served as an entrance, causing one of her fine leather gloves to fall out. Calling out to the lady, Kate bent down to pick up the fallen glove. As she stood up again, Kate was startled to see Rob walking towards them, at the exact same time a screeching of brakes could be heard, followed by a loud crashing sound as a car collided with a bus. The smaller vehicle spun across the road and onto the pavement, unceremoniously smashing into the tables set up outside the restaurant. The sound of breaking glass and screams confused the already shocked Kate, as she watched a slow-motion version of the accident unfolding in front of her eyes. The older lady was saved, whilst Rob was not. Having been thrown up into the air, he had landed heavily on top of the crashed car.

Kate screamed out in her sleep, startling the sleeping Pete, who woke up immediately and was now sitting bolt upright in bed. He gently shook Kate, trying to wake her up, whilst also reassuring her that she was okay and that it was just a dream. Obviously, not knowing what on earth she had been dreaming about and having been shocked out of sleep himself, although used to Kate's dreaming, Pete was feeling quite unnerved by her loud scream. As

Kate woke up and realised with relief that the accident wasn't real. Involuntary tears rolled from her eyes at the intensity of the dream and even as she snuggled into Pete's arms and he soothed her shaking body, it was a few moments before Kate could describe the awful scene. Feeling immensely grateful that Pete was there, Kate thanked him for waking her up and said she was going to get up and make herself a drink, then sit up for a bit to clear her head. Checking if she wanted him to get up with her, Pete didn't mind when she said no and that she just needed to do something to distract her mind. He knew the best thing was usually to leave her to read. It was often the only way she could avoid falling back into the same dream.

Making her way to the kitchen, Kate felt really shaken up by the dream and thought that maybe she should just check that Rob really was okay, then admonished herself for being silly, saying out loud that it *was* only a dream. Taking her cup of tea into the living room, Kate switched on a lamp before settling into her favourite armchair and picking up the book she'd started three days ago, but, unable to concentrate, she soon put it down again. The car accident was really bothering her. What if something really had happened to Rob in real life? Is that why she had dreamt about him, or was it just the girls' talk that evening? Kate was driving herself mad over the irrational dream and switched on the TV, hoping that a late-night comedy show would distract her mind, but the scene which flashed onto the screen was from a gruesome horror movie with blood, guts and gore oozing from someone's butchered body. Quickly turning the TV off again, Kate gulped her tea, feeling grateful for the warm comfort her favourite mug offered her. Needing to distract her mind, she decided to call her friend Lowry, who, being airline staff, was often in a different time-zone and would likely be awake to chat and tell Kate she wasn't going mad and that it really was just a bad dream. The other reason for choosing Lowry was that coincidentally she also knew Rob's family quite well and would likely know if anything was wrong. Lowry and Rob's sister had been at university together and became firm friends. Which also meant that Lowry had stayed over at Rob's Parents' house on more than one occasion during their university breaks, so had ended up knowing Rob quite well.

The telephone was on its fourth ring before Lowry picked up the call. "Hey Kate, how're you doing? Long time no speak, mate, but, what are you doing calling me in the middle of the night?" Lowry was in America and knowing the late hour for Kate, was concerned that something must be wrong.

"I'm fine thanks, Lowry, just having a bad-dream-night again, so I thought I'd grab the opportunity to call someone who would still be up." Kate laughed.

"Oh, I see, just a *convenient* night-time call then, is it?" Lowry didn't really mind the reason for Kate's unexpected call, she was always glad to hear from her university buddy. "So, what's new then, why the bad night, are you and Pete okay?"

"Oh, we're fine, Lowry, I just had a very weird dream though and it really unsettled me."

"Another bad dream huh, I remember you having a few of those at uni, you used to scare the bejesus out of me sometimes." Lowry remembered several occasions when Kate's bad dreams had totally unsettled her. She had soon learned to be adept at calming her friend down, usually, by making her recount the dream and then cracking a funny joke or two, about whatever scenario it was, making the whole thing sound so ridiculous that Kate was able to quickly dismiss it and move on.

"So, my friend, what was the dream about this time?" Reassuringly, Lowry sounded like her usual empathetic self to begin with, so Kate told her about Rob being killed. This time, Lowry was intrigued, wondering why Rob had suddenly cropped up in her dream. Kate explained about the evening chatter with the girls so that Lowry was soon on the same page.

"Wow, well, that'll do it mate, all men who let you down deserve to have a car thrown at them!" Lowry chortled and as Kate joined in, her involuntary laughter forced a lighter mood.

As the girls caught up on their news, the time flew by and Kate eventually said she'd best let Lowry go and get back to Pete. Thanking her friend for calming her down, with promises of speaking again soon, Kate said her goodbyes.

Turning off the living room lamp, Kate smiled at Lowry's banter as she walked back through to the darkened bedroom, now feeling much more relaxed. Pete wasn't even aware of her presence as she slipped between the sheets and snuggled up to him again. Sleep came quickly and so did Kate's dreams, but this time they were normal; her mind just reorganising its filing cabinets, whilst flinging random thoughts together. None of which joined up or made any sense at all.

When Kate woke up a few hours later, Pete was already in the bathroom. He needed to drive down to the south coast to start a planned maintenance schedule for four rescue helicopters, which meant he would be away for a week. Kate got up to make them both some breakfast and shouted out 'Morning Pete,' as she passed the bathroom door.

"Morning, gorgeous, I'll only be about ten minutes," Pete called back as he stepped into the shower.

"Okay, I'll make some tea and bacon rolls." Kate knew Pete's weakness for bacon on white bread, with real butter and a generous helping of HP sauce and smiled at his reply from behind the closed door.

"Oh, you're a star! Thanks babe. I'll be right there."

On the other side of the bathroom door, Pete was grinning at the thoughtfulness of his girlfriend, whilst also thinking, *she's a keeper, that one*. As he toyed with the idea of spending his life with Kate, Pete thought how the past few months of living with her had been the best of his life. Already feeling like the luckiest guy on earth to have met and fallen in love with Kate, he was still amazed that she loved him back so completely. Kate was everything he wanted in a woman, sexy, funny, honest, kind and very thoughtful, Pete realised he loved her very much and, in that moment, decided that when he got back from this trip, he was going to ask her to marry him.

Completely unaware of her boyfriend's intentions, Kate busied herself in the kitchen preparing breakfast for them both and feeling happy that she had also booked the day off to meet up with Inga. After their girls' night at Antoine's, Inga had asked to meet for lunch to talk through some of the issues she felt were damaging hers and Damien's relationship.

Knowing that whilst Damien's work was a massive part of the problem, it was also something Inga could not share in too much detail, so, she would have to choose her words carefully when talking to Kate.

Kate knew that Inga and Damien had been having some problems and felt honoured that Inga felt comfortable enough to confide in her, although she wondered whether she could offer any nuggets of wisdom that would help her friend. *Well, only time would tell*, Kate mused, then, calling to Pete that breakfast was ready, she carried it through to the table.

Chapter 3

A Wedding Anniversary to Remember

To celebrate their upcoming wedding anniversary, Inga had planned a surprise mini break for her and Damien at a fabulous and very expensive hotel. The package she had found included a visit to a nearby and very famous vintage racing motor museum. This part of their break was a special treat for Damien, who, being a confirmed petrol-head, would be delighted with the surprise his wife had in store for him. More so, that it would follow le pièce de résistance. An evening of sexy fun involving dinner, champagne and some very high heels. Inga also planned to wear a stunning silk dress, with a scooped back and fine straps criss-crossing her otherwise completely naked body. Feeling very excited about the surprise, Inga hoped she and Damien would be able to reinvigorate their marriage during this romantic mini break. It needed to be an occasion he would remember forever, yet absolutely not expect.

The dress Inga had bought and hidden in her closet was one that Damien had never seen her in, nor probably ever imagined she would wear. When she first tried it on, she had felt like a million dollars. Inga was now imagining the scene and how the dress would fall to the floor gracefully, when her husband's very deft fingers slipped the straps from her naked shoulders. It was an evening Inga had been thinking about ever since she found that perfect dress in the city and she was beyond excited about wearing it for Damien. Usually her husband arranged their wedding anniversary celebrations, but this one was special and Inga had persuaded him to leave it with her, promising him there was no need to fret and that they would have a great time.

Intrigued by his wife's change in demeanour whenever their anniversary celebration was mentioned, Damien secretly fantasised about what she might have planned for the two of them.

Today though, she had arranged to meet Kate at a favourite restaurant, which was situated in the centre of town. Having arrived early, Inga sat waiting patiently for Kate to arrive, feeling grateful for her friend's flexibility and compassionate nature. Inga felt that Kate was a bit more worldly-wise than she was and always appreciated how discreet Kate was. A crucial factor for this particular discussion. Generally, Inga was quite private about hers and Damien's relationship, never wanting to reveal too much to other people, which was in part, due to the type of work he did, but tough times needed alternative actions and so she had given herself permission to share a few of her more intimate concerns.

Unbeknown to Kate and their other friends, Damien was not the typical sales executive who travelled a lot with his job, a story they had come to know well and share with anyone who asked. No, the real truth was, Damien had been a UK Government MI5 Agent for the past seven years. As you would expect, the work was often dangerous and occasionally kept him away from home. Often for odd days, but this time it had been a few weeks, which was putting a huge strain on his and Inga's relationship. All the 'away from home stuff' was never going to be healthy for any marriage, hence why she was worried about theirs. Things felt different this time and Inga had been wondering just how dangerous her husband's work was with his latest case. Generally, her concerns centred around the worry of never knowing when, or if, he would be coming home again, but this time she felt unnerved, the time was dragging and although Damien had been calling her regularly, unusually he had seemed really tense and almost awkward at times.

Whilst Damien could not experience the same worries that Inga inevitably had, he understood only too well the pitfalls of trying to have a normal life, whilst also working as an MI5 agent for the British Government. It was a subject that everyone he worked with was very aware of too and for many of them, lost relationships were an expected and almost accepted side-effect of the job. What did cause Damien stress was those occasions when he had to infiltrate specific groups, some of whom were so sharp that Damien had to be a hundred percent above his game, so as not to cause suspicion. This latest job demanded him to spend even more time away from Inga and their home than was usual, which he also realised had not helped their recently strained relationship. Damien knew Inga loved him and felt sure she knew how much he loved her too, but this job was something different and he knew he had been away from home for too long. Whilst he always tried to reassure her not to worry and often tried to make light of things, Damien knew that was all Inga did do when he was away, worry, and this time, he knew that even though she was unaware of it, there was great cause to be concerned. This job was very dangerous, in more ways than one, not only because it involved an extremely dangerous family, but because there was an added complication that Damien was struggling to manage.

Seeing Kate rushing across the square towards her, Inga smiled and waved, hugging her friend as Kate reached the table. It was a bright and sunny day and although not overly warm, the two of them decided to sit outside and enjoy the sunshine. The two friends quickly settled down, making themselves comfortable, whilst also discussing the worries that Inga was fretting over.

Relaying her anniversary weekend plans, Inga chatted enthusiastically about how much she hoped to reignite the spark between her and Damien. Which of late seemed to have dulled somewhat. Noticing how Inga's eyes sparkled whilst she shared her evening plans for 'the dress', Kate chuckled with a sense of wicked naughtiness and wished Inga the very best of luck for the fabulous weekend she had so carefully planned. Knowing the hotel that they were staying in and how expensive it was, Kate also knew Damien was in for a real treat. Just a few more days and he would be back from his sales trip and ready to be wooed by his beautiful wife.

The two friends chatted for the best part of three hours and by the end of it, Inga admitted she felt much better, almost relieved, definitely calmer and much more positive. Naturally, she had taken great care *not* to share the truth about Damien's real job.

Meanwhile, having agreed on their safe place to talk, Damien was updating Mike Day, his MI5 boss. The two men were discussing the very worrying complications which had developed with the Mafia family that Damien was infiltrating. The daughter of the Don had taken a shine to Damien, or as she knew him, James. It had become an extremely dangerous situation and Damien was concerned; he didn't want to blow his cover, but he also couldn't allow the infatuation to grow. It was a tough situation. They were close to bringing the gang down and with so much at stake, Damien was being encouraged by Mike not to walk away and to do whatever it took to maintain his cover. Damien was not happy, he knew that Inga would leave him if he cheated on her and yet if he refused the attentions of the daughter – Simona – the Don would likely have him killed. The stakes were high and the value of the deal ran into the millions. Drugs and guns were what this underground operation were running and to put them out of business would be a massive achievement for the team. Mike pointed out that it would also see Damien being promoted and running his own team, which would take him out of immediate front-line danger. That little fact was something Damien knew Inga desperately wanted to happen, and soon, but this risk was too much. The personal price to him was very high and he needed to stall for time, to figure out how best he should handle Simona.

Mike suggested they find a way to remove 'James' from the job for a few days, so that Damien could join his wife for their wedding anniversary. Damien had been keen not to miss the long-planned-for weekend away with his wife and so his storyline with the gang was to be dramatised sufficiently for him to be away for a few days. Mike Day advised Damien to also take this free time to think about how he should handle Simona on his return. Damien was torn, but relieved to have a few days thinking time. He was missing Inga and needed the comfort of her arms around him, if only to maintain his sanity. But, he also knew that the scenario he was supposed to come up with to cope with Simona was beyond his current comprehension and that worried him even more.

Inga was excited, the day of their trip had finally arrived and Damien was home and upstairs getting changed before they set off for the hotel. A journey, she assured him, which would take no longer than two hours. Damien was intrigued by what lay in store, obviously still completely unaware of the surprise trip to the motor museum, or of the special dinner being prepared for all of the hotel's guests. Today was their actual anniversary and as luck would have it, when making their reservation, the staff had advised Inga that it was to be a black-tie occasion and so she had already packed the clothes that Damien would need, whilst she of course, planned to wear *the dress*.

Damien was impressed as they pulled into the gravelled entrance of the hotel, with its tree-lined driveway, which continued around the building into a very cleverly disguised car park. As it was late afternoon, they decided to go straight to their room to unpack and freshen up before dinner. The hotel footman opened the door into their room and Damien was surprised again, walking into what was actually a huge and absolutely delightful suite. It was the stuff of movies and made their anniversary feel even more romantic. A bottle of chilled champagne was already waiting for them as they entered. The footman, having carried their bags up as they checked-in, had introduced himself as Charles and offered his services, should they need them, on speed dial 55, via the telephone by the bed. Damien thanked him and paid a handsome tip, feeling very impressed by the fabulous hotel that Inga had brought him to. As the footman closed the door behind him, Damien immediately took Inga into his arms, pausing to take in the beauty of her face as his fingers reached to gently brush her cheek, he lifted her chin to look deep into her eyes. Feeling very aware of the love between them, Inga melted as the warmth of her husband's breath passed over her lips and passion took over, his kiss crushing hers. Inga felt as if he were kissing her for the very first time. Whilst Damien, overwhelmed by the whole sense of occasion was, in that moment, full of love and wanting for his incredible wife.

As they finally pulled apart, Inga was delighted, her plan was already working far better than she could have hoped. Watching Damien pour them both a glass of champagne, Inga almost whispered her love, "Damien, this moment, this place, us, you. Oh my darling, I love you so much."

As he walked towards her, offering champagne for her to take from him, Damien caught Inga's free hand and kissed her fingertips as he replied, "You are the most beautiful woman a man could wish for and I am very lucky to have the honour of calling you my wife."

Tears of happiness instantly sprang into Inga's eyes and as Damien kissed them away, he added, "I love you very much my darling, more than ever before."

An uncontrollable fresh tear escaped and Inga blushed, then smiled, before taking a sip of champagne and somewhat seductively, through shining eyes, she told him, "This is the most perfect evening my darling, just being here with you, in this moment and for what is to come later." Inga could barely contain herself.

Damien was excited and intrigued by that thought and his anticipation grew even more when Inga explained they needed to dress for a formal dinner and that his clothes were in the suit carrier, now hanging in the bedroom closet. Following Inga's instructions and walking through to the bedroom, Damien felt very aroused by the excitement that was oozing out of Inga; she was like a temptress and Damien was loving it. This was indeed going to be a very special night. Damien could feel an escalating buzz of sexual tension as he stepped into the shower. Enjoying the sensation of the hot water running down his muscular frame and already hardening, he imagined making love to his beautiful Inga when they returned to their room much later.

Having dressed in his dinner suit, Damien felt good and as he walked out of the bedroom Inga gasped and smiled. Her husband looked so very handsome and she loved every part of him. Intense sexual anticipation and romantic love filled the room and Inga had to walk away from Damien after the briefest of encounters, unable to keep her hands off him any longer. Inga knew without a doubt, that if she had even attempted to kiss her husband again, they would not make it downstairs for dinner.

Taking the champagne which Inga handed to him, Damien kissed her hand and mulled over what he wanted to do to her when they returned from dinner. Embellishing his thoughts, he watched the now giggling Inga walk through to the bedroom, glass of champagne in hand. Damien hardened again and turning towards the fireplace, he relished the effect Inga was having on him. As he watched the dancing flames flickering in the grate, Damien realised this had to be the honeymoon suite; every whim and want had been catered for, including the gas log fire. Damien acknowledged to himself that Inga had absolutely surpassed his expectations for this anniversary. Yet little did he know what was still to come.

A short while later, Damien heard the adjoining doors click open and turned to watch his wife walk through from the bedroom. Gasping at his smiling Inga, Damien acknowledged that she was a vision of loveliness. The sight of her in that absolutely stunning dress, which he had never seen before, had his passion rising and standing to attention for the third time that evening. Damien crossed the floor and stood in front of her, absorbing every ounce of the deliciousness that she oozed. He wanted her there and then. But, knowing they had just a short while before they were expected downstairs, he controlled his passion and instead, Damien beamed at her, telling her again how incredibly beautiful she was and that he could not believe this moment was real. Taking both of her hands, he raised them to his lips and kissed Inga's fingertips before pulling her towards him and kissing her more passionately than he even had before. Inga could feel Damien's excitement and wanted to reach down to touch him, but, like her husband, she too resisted and instead, returned his kiss just as passionately, telling him that she loved him, now and forever. There was a knock on the door and startled, the two of them separated, laughing at the idea of being caught in such an intense moment of passionate wanting. Opening the door, Damien stepped to one side as a dozen red roses appeared. He had, on checking-in, slipped a note to the reception staff, asking for an urgent delivery of red roses to surprise his wife. The hotel staff had got onto it immediately and somehow managed to achieve the request. It was Inga's turn to be surprised and utterly delighted at such a romantic gesture. As the flowers were set down and the footman retreated discreetly, Inga thanked Damien and stood looking at this most handsome of men, thankful that he was there and that he was hers. Naughty thoughts filled both their minds and quickly finishing their glasses of champagne, they agreed that perhaps they should go downstairs, before they missed dinner altogether.

The handsome young couple entered the grand dining room. Several pairs of eyes were upon them and a few intakes of breath could be heard as they admired the beautiful Inga and her dashing husband, now being shown to their candlelit table. Neither Inga nor Damien could feel any happier, this was a very special moment in their lives, precious beyond belief. The ambience, along with the exceptional service, was just like being in a movie and the exquisite food which followed could only be described as utterly divine. Damien and Inga were completely absorbed by one another. It was as if this evening were one of the earliest moments in their life together.

The warmth of the occasion and after-dinner drinks being offered were very tempting, yet whilst neither wanted this part of the evening to end, their passion was growing and both wanted to return to their suite, each feeling desperate to make love to the other. Extending the moment, they waited a little longer, allowing their passion to intensify. As the last sip of their drinks were taken, the two of them stepped onto the small dance floor. The band were playing a very romantic song, which fitted their occasion perfectly. Damien enjoyed showing off his beautiful Inga and as he took her in his arms and danced with her, his hand moved down her slim body. Feeling the warmth of her bare skin beneath the thin fabric which scooped low, exposing her naked back, Damien loved that Inga was his. This beautiful woman, who he was lucky enough to call his wife, oozed sex appeal, causing Damien to hold her even closer. His passion was barely controllable. Feeling grateful for the long line of his dinner jacket, as the song they were dancing to came to an end, Damien whispered his wanting need of her, suggesting they retire to their room. Inga was very aware of the effect she was having on her husband and felt as if she were in seventh heaven. Full of desire herself, she took Damien's hand as the two of them left the grand dining room. The same pairs of eyes were watching them as they passed through the exit of the hotel's exclusive restaurant and into the luxurious foyer. The journey in the elevator seemed to take forever and as Inga squeezed Damien's hand tighter, he smiled his brightest smile and again lifted her fingers to his lips, pressing a kiss onto them that told her everything she needed to know.

As the door to their suite clicked shut behind them, Damien followed Inga to the middle of the room, admiring her hips as they gently swayed with each step. Never before had he seen such a sexy walk or wanted a woman so much. Standing behind her, expertly, he slipped the dress from her shoulders and watched the silky fabric as it slid down her lithe, naked body. He absorbed every ounce of her wantonness and as she turned to face him, her nipples were taut, tempting his lips to suck them into his mouth. One hand reached them first as he pulled her towards him with the other, crushing her mouth with a passionate kiss so intense, that he thought he might burst. Inga was swept away by his love and desire for her and pulling away from him, standing in just her heels, she asked him to undress. Watching his every move as he slipped off his jacket and threw it aside, then pulling his bow tie undone, Inga smiled seductively as he released his belt to pull the shirt tails from his trousers. Within seconds, Damien was also completely naked. His glorious wanting passion for Inga was very evident, now stood to attention and rock hard with desire for the woman who stood in front of him. Taking her into his arms again, Damien pressed his hardness against her abdomen as he told her he wanted her, right here and right now. The two of them sank onto the floor in front of the fire and after pulling cushions from the furniture for Inga to lie against, Damien sucked her hard nipples into his mouth, toying with them both and driving Inga wild with desire for him. Knowing he could wait no longer, Damien lifted his beautiful, smiling Inga to sit astride him as, holding her hips with his hands, he repeatedly rode up into her, watching her breasts as they bounced with every demanding and wanting thrust. Inga was already close to orgasm and loving watching the obvious pleasure on Damien's face. Their groans could be heard in the corridor outside, as the intensity of passion overtook their senses and exploded, "Oh... my... god... Ingaaa..." Damien was so in love with his wife at that moment that he didn't care who heard him, or who knew. Inga's love for him was bursting from her heart as she climaxed again and again, never wanting to stop as she rode him hard, enjoying every clenching spasm that wracked her body, until they both flopped back on the cushions, exhausted but fulfilled. Damien's fingers were unable to resist touching her nipples as he caressed her skin in the firelight, before allowing his hands to explore the warm wetness that he had just filled her with, pushing his fingers into her and willing his passion to rise again, so he could once more take possession of his beautiful wife.

Chapter 4

The Morning After

Damien and Inga had spent half of the night by the fireside, before moving to the sumptuous bed and as they awoke that morning, each told the other how much they loved them. Neither one of them could be happier. Both felt like this had been the most perfect wedding anniversary that they had ever had. Having their breakfast brought to the room added to the occasion and as Damien went to answer the knock of the door, dressed only in the hotel robe, Inga sat up in their bed, eager to enjoy their relaxing morning together and once again make love to her husband.

As he opened the door, Damien's smile turned to shock and horror when he realised it was not a waiter carrying their breakfast. No, it was the very beautiful Simona stood facing him, with the biggest smile on her face and the sexiest of dresses barely covering her body.

"Why, James darling, you should have told me you were planning a little break, I could have joined you last night!" Simona teased him as she stepped forward to kiss Damien. His brain was racing to think of how he could explain this away to both Simona and Inga, whilst also not blowing his cover. Panicking inside and wondering how on earth she had known he was there, he needed an out. Simona was able to explain it herself though. Having been at the Spa-hotel overnight with a girlfriend, Simona's driver had spotted 'James' walking into the elevator after dinner, although, thankfully, he had not spotted the lady who had stepped into the same elevator a second earlier.

Simona had spent the night with her girlfriend, explaining with a wink to 'James' how she enjoyed the sexual company of both female and male friends.

Thankfully, Inga could not hear what was being discussed on the other side of their suite and was oblivious to the fact that Simona was, at that very moment, reaching inside her husband's gown to pleasure his already hard member.

"Oh James, I see you are ready for me darling. Won't you invite me in?"

Damien could see Simona's nipples pressing against the thin fabric of the dress restricting them and could not deny her beauty, or the sexiness of her body. Knowing Inga was waiting for him though and expecting their breakfast, Damien tried to get rid of Simona, whilst being very aware of her hands now caressing his extremely hard cock. Trying his best to pull away, Damien struggled, her hands just felt so good.

"Simona, this is an unexpected surprise. Ermm... I was actually just about to shower and dress. I have an urgent appointment to get to." Thinking on his feet, Damien made an obvious excuse, whilst simultaneously feeling unable to comprehend the shock of Simona not only standing in front of him, but that she looked red-hot and was still caressing his now rigid and about-to-explode cock. Inadvertently, he took a step back as Simona dropped to her knees and wrapped her mouth around him, sucking hard enough to make him groan. Damien felt a rush of forbidden pleasure fill his veins and without thinking, he pushed in deeper, loving the sensation of her warm mouth and tongue, as it flicked across the end, teasing out the already running juices. Unable to control himself any longer, Damien exploded into the wanting mouth of the beautiful temptress knelt before him, holding her head against him, as unthinking, he thrust

31

deeper into her throat, groaning with relief and disbelief. Suddenly, returning to his senses, he looked down at Simona as she withdrew and smiled up at him, his sperm having been swallowed and obviously enjoyed. Quickly lifting Simona up from the floor, Damien pretended to be shocked and suggested her father might not appreciate what she was doing to him. Simona laughed and grabbed hold of his balls, as her salty lips kissed him passionately, pressing her hard nipples against his now bare chest, before suddenly turning and walking away, sexiness oozing from her every pore as she left Damien wanting more.

Hurriedly closing the door, Damien stood stock-still for a moment, swiftly tying the gown back around him while he paused to gather himself. Feeling anxious as to how much Inga might have heard, Damien strode across the room, only to find that his luck was in. Inga was already in the bathroom, freshening up for the next stint of love-making with her gorgeous husband. As she opened the door, Inga smiled and walked across to him. Reaching to undo his gown whilst watching for his manly reaction, she expected to find him hard and wanting; her heart sank with disappointment on seeing that he was deflated and flaccid.

Damien was feeling slightly panicked at how he could escape this moment and leave their suite with Inga, without being spotted by Simona. Guilt flooded his mind as Damien's concern switched to Inga's safety; he could handle himself, but with these people, he knew that Inga's life could be snuffed out in the blink of an eye.

"Darling, let me go and freshen up for you." Damien wondered if Inga could smell Simona's perfume, but it seemed that the unsuspecting Inga was already familiar with the scent, which she also wore, so her senses did not react.

Feeling a little disappointed, but not wanting to spoil the moment, Inga responded with, "Okay, well we need to eat our breakfast before it gets cold anyway."

Naturally, Inga expected to find the food already set out on the table in their suite's sitting room. But, as Damien started walking into the huge bathroom he replied, "Oh, it wasn't breakfast honey, it was some random woman, looking for another guy that she'd picked up last night in the bar. To be honest she still seemed a bit tipsy to me. I couldn't get rid of her." The explanation he offered was the best he could come up with that was also as close to the truth as possible. Damien hated lying to Inga, but more so, he hated that he had enjoyed Simona's mouth so much that he'd not been able to control his exploding cock. Closing the door behind him, Damien promised to only be a few minutes. Staring at his own reflection in the mirror over the wash basin, Damien breathed deeply, not quite sure how he'd managed it, but relieved that he seemed to have pulled off what must be the best and worst situation for a man to find himself in. Splashing water over his face and then his cock, Damien wondered how he could get Inga safely out of the hotel; he knew she was expecting him to make love to her, but he also knew they had to leave and very soon! Quickly brushing his teeth, Damien returned to their bed, where Inga was already waiting for him, aroused and full of wanting. Damien loved Inga and cursed Simona for spoiling their amazing weekend. As he took his wife into his arms again, he told her how much he loved her and how much she meant to him. A mountain of guilt was building inside him, but, as Inga responded warmly and she reached for the hardness that she was used to, she began coaxing him, her kisses working down his body until her tongue could flick and tease Damien enough that he peaked again, desperate to enter her wet, wanton, softness. Damien groaned as he remembered Simona's lips and mouth sucking him hard, as he now thrust inside Inga, again and again, loving every inch of her, yet ridden with guilt at his fantasised thoughts of Simona. Inga cried out as her orgasm took hold and Damien exploded inside her again, how was this even possible? What had Simona done to him? His passion was finally spent and his mind was blown. Damien knew he needed to find a reason for them to leave and get to the car, without Simona or her driver spotting them and without alerting Inga to the danger. It was an impossible situation. The only option was an emergency 'work' call. As Inga left their bed again and headed for the bathroom, Damien sent the emergency coded message via his mobile phone.

Ten minutes later, Damien received a call and, already dressed, he called out to Inga that they needed to leave urgently, explaining that his cover was apparently compromised and for safety reasons, he was being instructed for them both to leave the hotel immediately. Inga was shocked, confused and angry. Why, on this special weekend, did Damien's work have to come first?

"It's for our safety, my darling." Damien was trying to pacify his now desperately sad wife. "This is a different type of case to normal and the stakes are extremely high, we should have been safe, but I guess they're being overly cautious because they know how much you mean to me."

The thought, *thou dost speak with forked tongue*, raced through his mind and even though Damien knew part of what he had said was true, the other part was the pretence that he hated most. More lies and more deceit of his beloved Inga, but, he also knew he loved her more than the worry of the lies, so he had to protect her first and pay the consequences for his earlier weakness, later.

As Inga repacked her beautiful dress into their bag, a tear escaped and the wonderful loving mood they had experienced since they arrived felt utterly trashed. Inga was heartbroken, fearing her marriage would not survive the sticky times they'd had recently.

Damien was back in work-mode, checking the corridor was empty, before instructing Inga to go straight to their car with her bag and to drive home alone. Damien knew he could not risk being seen with Inga, because that would put her life in danger. Telling her not to worry and that he would sort out the final bill, Damien explained that another car would be waiting to take him home separately.

Inga started to cry, having realised the seriousness of the situation and kissing Damien goodbye, she left the room alone. Watching tears escape from those beautiful eyes killed Damien and whilst he waited five more minutes, he wanted to kick something. Damien was angry with himself for his betrayal of Inga and angry that her wonderful plans had been ruined.

Knowing their bill would have already been settled, Damien managed to find his way out of the hotel without bumping into Simona, or her driver. Now, sat in the back of the waiting car, he told his own driver to leave, thanking him at the same time. It was all meant to look like he'd been collected by a private taxi, in case spying eyes were watching. Safely out of the hotel grounds, Damien called their home phone and left a voice message for Inga to pick up when she got home, knowing he would be called in for a debrief and would not be able to call again until the following day. Their special weekend was ruined and Damien blamed himself. Wondering if Inga would ever forgive him, Damien silently prayed that she would as he left her the most loving message and apology that he could. He could not bear to lose her.

Inga arrived home, her face red and swollen from the tears that she'd cried as her heart felt like it would break.

Seeing the answering machine flashing at her, she picked up Damien's message and her heart sank even further. How could this wonderful weekend and last night have gone so horribly wrong? Unable to unpack her bag, Inga left it in the hallway and made her way upstairs to their bedroom. As she undressed and walked through to their shower, Inga was oblivious of the armed protection already in place outside the house, now watchful for her safety. After all, this was a mafia gang they were dealing with and they knew only too well what could happen.

Inga ran a hot shower, needing to wash the sadness away and as she stood under the running water she worried what would happen to their marriage, feeling certain that Damien's work would eventually take its toll, as it had with so many others in the team. Remembering the promise Damien made to her on their wedding night, Inga felt reassured that he would not willingly let that happen, but still, the negative voice in her head said, *'Yes, but, it's unwillingly, that is what will happen and how it will end.'* Tears ran down her face once again, as sadness overcame her body, now racked by heaving sobs.

The past few months of Damien working undercover with the mafia had taken its toll on the both of them and Damien had indeed been different with her, often being a bit sharper than he would normally be, in his tone and attitude. But, last night, Inga felt like she had the old Damien back, the man she had loved and married, and the man that she still wanted to grow old with. *But where is he now*? Inga wondered.

In truth, Damien was having to relay everything that had happened to Mike and two of his superiors, in every embarrassing and personal detail. One of his superiors initially joked about Simona's actions and how that was every man's fantasy, but quickly changed tack as he saw the anger flash across Damien's face as he demanded that this could not and *must* not be allowed to leak! Simona was work and his betrayal of Inga was inexcusable and already eating him up inside. Knowing the only reprieve from the guilt would be to confess to her, Damien also knew that he could never tell her, because she would leave him and never forgive him, especially given the occasion.

Damien knew he would have to carry the burden of his guilt forever and accepted it to be a rightful punishment. Decisions were made on how best to continue undercover and it was decided that this had been the closest of chances, but that all seemed to be well, so a story was invented to back up the meeting Damien had told Simona he was due to attend. Damien was then advised to go home for one more night, with good luck wishes to try and repair some of the damage with Inga.

It was very late by the time Damien returned home and Inga was already asleep in bed. The protection detail had informed him that whilst all had been quiet, Inga had not even left the house since returning home that morning. What they didn't tell him was that they had enjoyed watching her walk naked back and forth across the bedroom, via the floor to ceiling windows, which, from their elevated cover position, made it an easy view. A perk of the job was how they thought of it, whilst also knowing that Damien would want to seriously hurt them if he knew. The two men had convinced each other that it wasn't their fault, after all, they'd been instructed to remain inconspicuous and ensure that Inga did not suspect she had a protection detail watching her.

Damien crept into the bedroom and pulled the curtains closed, knowing there were eyes prying; he did not want them to watch him comforting Inga. Leaning over his sleeping wife, he kissed Inga's forehead before walking into their bathroom to shower and clean his teeth; he wanted to feel clean enough to touch his wife, a woman he considered to be pure and innocent. How Damien would ever feel clean enough though, after what Simona had done to him, he did not know. Not that he had much option than to go along with her desires. Although, he also knew he didn't *have* to leave his rampant cock in her mouth until he shot his load. Damien cursed himself again.

As he returned to their marital bed and slipped between the covers, Damien put his arms around Inga, whispering how sorry he was and that he loved her more than life itself. Inga felt Damien getting into bed and waited for his touch, before responding sadly with the question that had been burning through her mind all day, "Is this it Damien? Is this our life forever?"

Damien's own heart ripped apart at the pain he had caused her and he promised that things would change after this case; knowing his promotion would mean he would not be undercover again, which meant Inga would be safe and they could live a more normal married life. But, Damien also knew, it was a story that many at work had told their loved ones, only to have hopes dashed, as circumstances changed. Holding Inga tighter, he felt her body relax as exhausted sleep took over her mind again; his own in turmoil over his guilt and how to be a better husband and protect his beloved Inga.

Chapter 5

Afraid to Tell

Inga knew she could not tell Kate or the others what had happened, because they didn't know what Damien really did for a living and of course, she could never tell them that he was a spy, because his life depended on it. Not only that, she'd had to sign the Official Secrets Act herself before he was even allowed to marry her.

When they first started seeing each other and then became more serious about their relationship, Damien had to seek permission to tell Inga about his real job. It was something he wanted to do as soon as he could, knowing how he felt about her and how important it was to explain the pitfalls of being in a serious relationship with someone like him, especially because she could NEVER tell anyone what he really did for a living. Damien was very clear in explaining how, in his business, loose lips really did risk lives. Which in this instance, at the very least, would mean his life and possibly hers too; it was something he had drummed into Inga and despite loving him, she had wondered at her own capabilities of carrying that knowledge and not talking to ANYONE about it. Finally, Inga realised that carrying such a secret alone was absolutely necessary, because she too had totally and utterly fallen in love with Damien and had known she wanted to spend her life with him. So, somehow, whilst not knowing quite how, she had begun that arduous journey of bearing the weight of such knowledge. Which meant that now, in this moment and despite her anguish, she had to do the very same thing and keep quiet. The shock and pain of it all, was almost too much to bear.

Having woken early and already needing to go back into his undercover role, Damien told Inga he loved her very much, explaining that whilst there would be no more breaks until the job had ended, which they expected to happen in two to three weeks, he promised faithfully to make it up to her when this was all over. Unsure of how she now felt, Inga promised to wait and agreed they should talk when this job was all over.

Whilst Damien knew the big shipment was due, the Don and his closest protectors were being cagey about final dates. Which was expected but also hugely frustrating to Damien and the MI5 team. Now back in the guise of James, Damien had not seen Simona since he'd got back three days ago. A sense of intrepid concern filled his mind as he hoped she would be discreet and not disclose their little encounter to anyone, especially her father. The Don's men regarded Simona as forbidden fruit, despite secretly enjoying her titillating behaviour; each of them had, at one time or another, watched Simona and fantasised about her very sexy body, imagining what they would do to her and how inappropriate, yet exciting it would be to have her. All except Damien. That was, until their little encounter, but, now he too found himself fantasising about Simona and her mouth sucking his cock. Despite knowing her type and the very real dangers involved in this instance, Damien comforted himself with the thought that he loved Inga. Yet he still had to force the memory of Simona's soft, warm mouth from his mind. Which was something he began to find himself needing to do more often than he should.

Despite being twenty-three, Simona was perfectly old enough to do as she pleased, but being concerned about how her father would react, she had never told him of her bisexuality. It was a well-known fact among those around Simona, that her father still regarded her as pure, a virgin, just waiting for the right man to come along. Only Leon, her trusted driver and bodyguard, knew different and he would never tell, for fear his own life would be snuffed out. Besides which, Leon had long ago decided that should the truth ever be revealed, he would plead no knowledge of her sexuality. That piece of information could only ever result in a no-win situation for him. Therefore, keeping quiet was the price he had to pay to ensure continued receipt of the huge salary the Don bestowed upon him. A salary which provided well for his family and assured reasonable security for their future. Whilst Leon was not prepared to die just yet, he also knew he could be gone at any time and without warning. It was a high price to pay, but Leon loved his family and wanted to provide for them. Besides which, he also knew too much and was in too deep. No way would the Don allow him to walk away easily, he was sure of that. Leon knew he was too good at his job and that both Simona and the Don trusted him implicitly.

Whilst Simona often flirted and toyed with her father's men, she did so in a way that ensured they all thought of her as a woman who would only give herself to the right man. Privately though, she did not know if she would ever be able to choose between a man or a woman as her lifelong partner. When that moment finally arrived, Simona felt sure she would know who truly was 'the one'. Meanwhile, she would pick and choose her lovers for as long as possible, until that special someone swept her off her feet, be they male or female. One thing Simona did know was, seeing James at the hotel in just his robe had turned her on so much that she wanted to conquer him. Which is exactly what she had done when she dropped to her knees and took him into her mouth. Enjoying that James was so turned on that he couldn't resist her, as he pushed into her mouth again and again, had made Simona very happy. But now, she wanted to feel him inside her and she was already secretly scheming on how to achieve that reality – it would have to be somewhere private – Simona did not want her father or any of his men to know about her lust for James.

Unaware of Simona's plans, Damien kept up his undercover role, knowing the next two weeks were key; he had provided detailed information to his superiors and everyone was on stand-by. The deal was red-hot and ready to be taken. But, despite being just two weeks away, Damien was now more concerned at how he could avoid Simona for those two weeks; she was dangerous, both to him and the planned raid his team were working on.

Meanwhile, back at home, Inga went about her usual activities, including keeping her weekly date with the girls and answering all of their questions about the big anniversary weekend. Kate especially wanted to know what Damien thought of the dress. Inga had thought through the storyline a dozen times and now described how the evening had gone, only hinting at how they had made love in front of the fire for hours – leaving her legs feeling like jelly the next morning – until Damien had answered that telephone call. Inga fed the girls with enough titillation so they would knowingly understand how well it had gone, without pressing her about the morning-after activities. Thankfully, none of the girls asked her about the motor museum trip, so Inga didn't have to invent a story about that.

Kate was hard to fool though and was concerned that despite Inga's relaying of their wonderful weekend, the light in her eyes wasn't shining as brightly as it had done when the two of them had met for lunch. Kate silently wondered if maybe all was not quite as well as Inga was making out, but she did not press her, knowing that if Inga wanted to talk about it, she would, in her own time.

Anxious to steer the conversation away from herself, Inga asked how Pete's latest trip was going. Kate explained that he was going to be away for another couple of weeks but would then be taking a month off and that he'd suggested they go on holiday somewhere. All of the girls envied the idea of a month-long holiday and said so. Kate felt really excited about the idea herself and hoped for a romantic, tropical destination.

Inga breathed an internal sigh of relief as the chatter turned to Kate and Pete's potential holiday locations, the best sunny beaches, sunscreen and escaping the daily grind of work.

Damien was finding it difficult to avoid Simona, she seemed to be everywhere and he'd noticed that when nobody was looking at her, she would wink at him and smile seductively, offering a discreet view of her cleavage as she would lean forward, pretending to adjust something on her clothing. Simona's plan was to have enough of her breasts visible to torment him and keep his eyes on her. Knowing he was being watched, Damien was aware that Simona's distraction was one he had to force himself to avoid looking at. But boy, was she tempting, he had still not forgotten her soft warm mouth and whilst his mind constantly tried to push those thoughts away, his cock would not allow him to forget. Damien realised Inga would be devastated if she knew how Simona was invading his mind, but he couldn't control himself.

This was a job that he now wished he had never taken. Promotion and an easier future with Inga had been the drivers and now that he and his team were so close to nailing this massive deal, Damien knew he couldn't walk away, no matter how tricky the situation became. Instead, he had to focus on the job and temporarily stop thinking of Inga. As much as he loved her, worrying about her now, could trip him up and cost him his life.

"So, what do you think, James?" Damien had not heard the question from Leon.

"James!"

"What? Huh, sorry mate, I was miles away, what did you say?" Damien glanced across to Leon, Simona's driver and bodyguard. They were having coffee in the staff kitchen, whilst Simona and her father were having a private lunch out on the pool terrace.

The property was worth millions and was surrounded by high security fencing and cameras, offering the family the best of protection, whilst allowing them to enjoy living in the lap of luxury. Simona's own quarters were situated on the opposite side of the pool. It was a pretty summer house style building, with curtained glass doors, which ran the length of the pool. Even her bedroom had curtained doors opening onto the terrace.

Leon spoke again. "The Don's out tonight and not back for a couple of days. Simona is happy to stay home and suggested I take a couple of days off with my family. She said you could stay and protect her. She's speaking to her father about it over lunch."

Damien almost choked on his coffee.

Startled, Leon quickly asked, "You okay James, mate? Went down the wrong way eh?" But, at James' insistence that he was okay, Leon did not suspect that anything was wrong, other than James swallowing his coffee too quickly. The fact was, Leon had assumed that like the other men, James would have no qualms about driving and protecting the sexy Simona. Most of them would have given their right arm for the honour of spending close personal time with the Don's daughter; knowing that most of their time would be spent watching her bikini-clad body, sliding in and out of the pool, water running from her long, silky dark hair and dripping down her body as she walked up from the pool-steps and on towards her sunbed.

Damien had already witnessed many of those moments when sat around the pool with the Don and whilst he had admired Simona's beauty, he had never once thought anything sexual about her. Damien knew she liked him; being a handsome man, he was used to female attention − it was something he and Inga often joked about − but he loved Inga, she was his life, outside of this dangerous one and he had never previously been tempted by other women. Until now.

"Ermm, well, I guess if the Don wants me to, I can be available." Damien had no choice, he knew Simona would persuade her father and he could not reject the suggestion, the deal was too close to fruition. Mike Day had already suggested he might have to go along with anything that cropped up, to avoid blowing the deal. These men were murderous drug-dealers and heavily armed; they would have no qualms about killing one of their own, if they suspected an informant in their midst. Not only that, several of them were wanted for questioning in relation to three recent and unsolved gangland killings.

Damien knew he was on a hiding to nothing and that there was no way out of it, especially as the Don would be away for a few days and would want Simona looked after by someone he trusted. Changing the subject away from thoughts of driving and protecting Simona, Damien asked Leon what plans he had for his family over the next couple of days. Leon was careful with how much information he shared with James, because whilst he really liked the newest member of the Don's inner circle, he didn't know him well enough to share the truth. Which was that he was planning to take the time to relocate his family somewhere safe. It would be a stepping stone to them all moving thousands of miles away, to a different country. Following recent events, Leon felt sure it was only a matter of time before Simona's love-life led to his death, so he needed to get out soon and whilst the going was good – his plan was to quit working for the Don after the next drug-drop – but in truth, the only way to fully escape would be for him and his family to leave the country. Preferably leaving no trace of where they were headed to.

Realising his timing was precious, Leon had sown the seed with Simona about possibly taking a few days off, suggesting James stand in for him whilst her father was away. Simona reacted well and quickly realised what a stroke of luck it was to have this opportunity to have James to herself. Well, apart from the housekeeping staff of course, they would still be around, but that was normal for Simona, so it wasn't a consideration or worry.

Simona had pounced on Leon's suggestion and, in her excitement, said she would speak to her father at lunch that very day. Everything was falling into place for her and she was beyond giddy with excitement, whilst Damien was filled with impending doom, knowing he would have trouble on his hands being left alone with Simona. Inga played on his mind. He wanted desperately to speak to her, but, there was no opportunity. Radio silence was in place. Boss' orders.

Simona and her father had a pleasant lunch. The Don was in a good mood, knowing he was about to make millions. Not only that, his only daughter, his most precious and beautiful Simona, was on good form, happy and for a pleasant change, was not wanting to spend her free time in the city's nightclubs. Telling her father that she needed a few days to relax and wanting to take advantage of him and the men being out of the house, Simona convinced the Don to just leave James with her, adding that Leon deserved a few days off with his family. Besides, she added, James was a good driver and if she needed to go out, he was perfectly capable of driving and protecting her. Feeling happy at seeing Simona so relaxed and willing to stay home, the Don agreed. The older man really liked James and despite him having only been with them for five months, the Don felt he could trust James with his much-cherished daughter.

Damien had already gone outside and was stood by the cars when the Don summoned him, to advise that he was being trusted to watch over Simona, whilst he, the Don, was away. James was to protect her and drive her if she needed to go out for anything. The Don also reminded James that, short of his dear departed wife, Simona was the most precious person in his life. The pressure for Damien was well and truly ON.

"I won't let you down, boss. Don't worry, nothing will happen to her." Damien's insides were in knots, he was totally screwed. A bad feeling was growing inside him and he knew this was his punishment for that momentary lapse when he had cheated on his beautiful Inga. Damien shuddered; he knew he was in trouble, with a capital T!

Leon was ecstatic. His own plans were looking rosy as he thanked James for agreeing to watch Simona, then offered a few pointers as to what she liked to do and when to help her into the car and when not to. "Simona is very particular, James, so be careful to heed what I've told you."

Damien nodded. "Sure Leon, of course, no problem. You enjoy your time off." Having listened intently, whilst also trying to look interested, Damien was careful to take onboard everything Leon was saying, knowing none of it would be needed, because Simona had made it more than obvious that she wanted him and had no interest in going out.

Radio silence was now in place whenever Damien was at the Don's home, both to Inga and work, unless it was an emergency. Apparently, Simona sucking his cock did not breach the emergency rules as far as his boss was concerned. Unless of course, his wife happened to also be in the next room. A reference to the hotel of course and not that his boss expected Inga to be anywhere near the Don's home. But, there was no doubt, Mike Day's message had been loud and clear, if Simona wanted to suck James' cock again, he was to let her! Damien wasn't sure whether to feel angry or happy at that thought, however, he did feel immense guilt, knowing it was more than likely going to happen.

Chapter 6

Two Days

The Don and his entourage had only been gone for two hours when Simona made her first move. Having sat casually chatting and drinking with James as her father's entourage had driven away, Simona then left him sitting at the table on the terrace, telling him she wanted to swim. Aware of exactly what she was doing and had done whilst James had not been looking, Simona enjoyed having James to herself, to protect and entertain her, revelling in the knowledge that he was watching her every move, as she swam up and down the pool. Simona had spiked James' drink with a potent white powder, to ensure he was powerless to her charms and once that powder took effect, she knew she would have him.

Simona's usual daily swim was forty lengths of the pool, but this time she only swam twenty, before standing up in the middle. The water level was just above her bikini top, as she walked slowly towards the corner steps to gracefully emerge from the water, aware of the sun glistening on the droplets now running down her wet body. Simona's usual routine was to walk across to the sunbed and pick up the towel she always left on it, then gently squeeze the water from her hair before lying down to enjoy the feeling of the warm sunshine as it dried her wet skin. Damien expected her to follow the usual routine, but this time, Simona's wet footprints walked back towards him, her silky, dark hair shining as the sun's rays were captured by the water droplets running from the ends. Damien thought how perfect she looked. It was as if she had just stepped out of a modelling shoot. There was no denying it, her body truly was stunning and with the warm sunlight radiating over them both, he thought how Simona was easily every man's fantasy. It was obvious to any onlooker why the Don's men were all so turned on by her.

Now, standing in front of him, Simona asked Damien to tell Cook to prepare them lunch and then take the afternoon off, suggesting she need not return until it was time to prepare dinner. Eliza – their cook – was not used to such generosity from Simona, but she had learnt not to question any instruction from the Don, or his daughter, being used to leaving the house for long periods of time whenever the Don needed privacy. With lunch already prepared, Eliza was able to drive away from the house almost immediately and as she reached the big gates that protected the estate, she waved to the guard, who resumed his position after securing the entrance again.

Armand, the gardener, was the only other member of staff in the grounds that day, but he was busy working on the hedges. The small power-cutter he used could be heard periodically, as he meticulously trimmed the carved out shapes he had created over the years, at the Don's request. A loyal servant, the gardener had been with the Don since before Simona was born and his love for her was like that of a grandfather, which comforted the Don whenever he was away from home.

Damien liked Armand and knowing he truly was 'just the gardener' and in no way involved in the criminal behaviours of his master, Damien would occasionally join the older man, gleaning information about the family and the estate and how he had seen it change over the years. That information had been invaluable in building up knowledge of how the estate worked, including the points of access.

At Simona's request, Damien had waited to watch Eliza leave and now, as he walked back poolside, he expected to see Simona lying on her sunbed, but she was nowhere to be seen. A sense of concern began to rise in him as he called her name through the open doors leading into the main house.

Watching James from behind her curtained doors, Simona giggled, knowing he would be starting to worry about her. While his back was turned, she opened two of the doors, so he would assume she was obviously in her quarters. As Damien turned to glance across the pool towards Simona's accommodation, he felt irritated at her game-playing. Walking towards her rooms, his mind flipped to Inga and what she would be doing whilst he was babysitting a spoilt twenty-three-year-old. Damien started to feel annoyed; he knew this was a bad deal and he wanted out, but he was committed and knew he had to play along with Simona's silly games.

Glancing in through the open door, Damien could not see her, so he called out and then knocked loudly – there was no response – Damien assumed she must be showering and so he waited outside the door. The noise from the power-cutter suddenly stopped and Damien knew he had to be cautious; he didn't want Armand to see him outside Simona's rooms and get the wrong idea.

Simona was still nowhere to be seen and Damien could hear no noise, so he called out again, just to check she was in her bedroom.

"Simona, are you in there?"

"Oh, hi James, yes, I'm just going to have a quick shower." Simona's voice was innocent and lighthearted, which softened James' anger, as he cursed himself for thinking she was playing games. Then, just at that very moment, he heard a small scream, followed by a bump and reactively, he called out again, more urgently.

"Simona! Simona! Are you okay?"

There was no reply.

"Simona? I'm coming in!"

Bursting into the bathroom, Damien was shocked to find that Simona was indeed playing games with him. She had not fallen or injured herself and as he almost fell through the door, Simona quickly closed it behind him and turned the key to lock them both in. Dropping her towel as she did so, she now stood naked in front of him. Damien was shocked at her behaviour, yet also impressed by her stunning figure and his previous irritation quickly turned to concern, knowing that Armand could be walking around anywhere outside.

Keeping his voice low, Damien begged the question, "Simona, are you mad? What do you think you are doing?"

Simona looked at him with feigned hurt as she stepped towards him. The large walk-in shower was behind her and running at full pelt, causing the steam to slowly build up around them, now that the door was closed. Damien knew he was in big trouble. If he rejected her, she would likely tell her father he'd tried it on with her against her will and he would be killed. If he got caught by Armand, he would be reported and also killed. If he jeopardised the whole surveillance job, he would be killed career-wise and if Inga ever found out, he would lose her forever, and Damien loved her, really loved her. He didn't want this and his mind was swirling, as all of those thoughts spun around in his head. The heat of the steam and his involuntary attraction to Simona's nakedness caused a reaction in Damien, enabling the drugs to begin to take over, confusing his mind and inventing thoughts of having Simona for himself.

Simona stepped closer and started to undo his shirt.

"James, I want you, don't you want me?" She gazed up at him with puppy-dog eyes, as her fingers reached the final button.

"No, I mean yes, well, no, because your father will kill me." Damien was playing for time, panicking at what to do, wondering how to handle the dangerous situation he had landed himself in. Simona's hands slipped inside his shirt, tweaking his own nipples whilst hers hardened with lust for him. Damien was a red-blooded male and her perfect, naked body of wanton longing, was overwhelming his senses, along with the perfume she had liberally sprayed over herself. The wrongness of it all was also now, unwillingly, turning him on. He knew this was every man's fantasy, but he also knew it could leave him alone forever, or even worse, dead. Damien had no choice, knowing his life was at risk, but not only that, everything about this case was at risk!

Oh boy, did she know exactly what she was doing. Damien's head was spinning and he felt different, suddenly happier, more excited. The thrill was addictive and his lust was growing, suddenly he felt strong, masterful and extremely wanting for Simona's seductive sweetness.

Simona's hands reached out and she continued undressing him. Previously unwilling, Damien's anger and frustration had now completely turned to lust. He was hardening and growing bigger and she knew it. Laughing when his pants fell to the floor as she first undid his belt, then his fly, Simona was loving every minute of this. Damien always went commando, so there was nothing now to restrict his fully erect cock as Simona dropped to her knees and took him into her mouth. Damien groaned, her mouth felt so soft, so warm and wet, so... ohhh. As Damien shuddered, his senses were screaming and he found himself at the point of no return. Lust took over as he pushed further into her soft mouth and her tongue teased him again and again, licking along the length of his cock, before repeatedly taking in its fullness. Momentarily torn between lust and guilt, Damien withdrew from her mouth, but his passion was ready to explode and he wanted her, right now. There was no going back for him, as all thoughts of Inga were shut out of his mind and the intensity of the moment took over. Simona stood up and pulled him into the shower with her. The warm water cascaded over their naked bodies as Damien's hands searched for her hard nipples before he crushed her mouth with a passionate kiss; his cock had a mind of its own, reaching for her wetness, as his hands and mouth explored every part of her upper body, before moving down to feel every other inch of her, pushing his fingers inside her softness as his voice uttered the words quietly, but with intent, "Oh my God, Simona, you are so fucking horny, this is so wrong and I am totally screwed, but I really want you, right now and hard!"

Simona giggled. She was in control, she had him and now she wanted him as much as he wanted her. Playing with him, teasing him and holding his cock in her hand whilst rhythmically pulling on it, as he again pushed his fingers in and out of her, before spinning her around. Then pulling her to lean against him, he looked down at her naked breasts, as both of his hands reached around to cup them, squeezing her nipples until she cried out. The water was streaming over them both as Damien spun her around again, to face him and reaching a hand under each buttock, he lifted her up as they slammed against the wall. Damien's cock had never been so erect, nor had he ever felt so turned on by a woman and without using his hands, his cock found its way into her warm wetness as he slid her down onto it, causing her to gasp at the size of him. They were both close to peaking as Damien lifted her up, thrusting into her urgently again and again, until neither of them could hold back any longer. Simona sunk her teeth into his shoulder to stop herself screaming out, causing Damien to thrust violently into her as the pain from her teeth broke his skin and his cock fulfilled its purpose, exploding hot sperm inside her. Conjoined, they slumped against the wall, neither of them wanting to move, until Damien's cock softened and Simona slid off him, each clinging to the other as their legs jellified.

"Fucking hell, Simona, what have you done to me?" Damien was referring to the power of his orgasm as well as the teeth-marks in his shoulder.

"James..." Simona was breathless and her legs weak as she fell against him, reaching to turn off the water, "...you really have, well and truly, fucked me." Simona laughed and reached for her towel, stumbling as Damien simultaneously caught her before she fell. As she steadied herself, Simona looked deep into James' eyes, she had him and she knew it! The power drove her crazy and she stood on tiptoe pulling his face to her lips as they kissed a passionate after-sex-kiss. Damien was drowning in a sea of desire, lust and guilt, as Inga once again returned to his thoughts. But, still influenced by the drugs he pushed her memory out and kissed Simona harder, unable to stop the feelings that were surging through his body. *Oh, my God! This woman!* Damien had never felt this before, not even with Inga. His sexual passion was alight and he could not stop it, nor did he want to. Picking Simona up in his arms, he walked over to her bed and laid her on it. Pushing her legs apart, his mouth ventured down towards her most intimate of places, as he began kissing her, his lips and tongue exploring her softness. Simona's desires increased again and, holding his head firmly against her, she lifted herself up to meet his mouth as, seeking out her clitoris, his tongue flicked it again and again, causing Simona to moan with wanting and no longer caring who might find them. Damien found himself lost in lust. *What was going on with him? He had never been this horny!* His unrestricted lust was unaware of the drug that Simona had added to both of their drinks earlier, which was obviously working well for them both, because his cock was rock-hard again and wanting her wetness as much as his mouth had done, she too was ready for him again. As she came close to climax, Simona cried out his name, "James..." Damien flipped her over and pulled her thighs up to meet his cock, entering her easily as he thrust deep inside her. Simona was loving it, she knew the drug was working and she could keep going as long as James did. She was as turned on as he was and pushed against him, begging him to go faster, harder, deeper, as her hands simultaneously reached between her legs and she grabbed his balls. Damien couldn't stop.

"Fuuuuuuuucking hell Simona..!" Damien exploded inside her again, his orgasm lasting much longer than normal and that was it, right at that moment, he knew he wanted to fuck this woman forever!

Simona was biting the bed sheets, unable to speak as her climax squeezed James' cock again and again, wrenching every bit of his climax from him as hers took hold. Damien had never fucked anyone like this before and he could not believe it. Simona was his, totally his and no matter what anyone else did to her, nobody would ever fuck her again like this, except him. At least, that's what the drugs told him.

As their second climax subsided, Damien rolled her over and then lay on top of her, kissing her and telling her he loved her. *Oh my God, did he just say he loved her?* Yes. He did. *Damien thought he loved Simona, but what about Inga?*

What about Inga indeed. Damien didn't yet know that it was the drugs messing with his head. But, what he did know was that he had not only just fucked the Don's daughter, he'd also just told her he loved her! *What the hell was he thinking?* Damien didn't know and he didn't care, he just wanted to stay with this adorable woman.

Sexually exhausted, the two of them fell into post-sex sleep and stayed that way, until waking with a start, only to find the time was six p.m. *Cook would be back and the gardener would be in the kitchen with her!* Damien's head was only just clearing, as the final effects of the drug began to wear off and he looked across at the still sleeping form of Simona.

What the fuck had he done? He remembered their love making and the intensity of the lust he had felt for her, lust or love, no… yes… oh no, he had told her he loved her! Oh my God, Inga, what have I done?

Damien's head was spinning, the after-effects of the drug were unknown to him, so he didn't even realise what Simona had done, or that it had been the drugs which had pushed him into having such intense, exciting and passionate sex with her. *Yes, passionate sex, something he usually only did with Inga, but now, now he had screwed the Don's daughter and betrayed his beloved wife.* Damien wanted to punch something.

Simona's eyes opened and her hand reached up to stroke his back as Damien got up from the bed. "James, you were as wonderful as I knew you would be!" Simona almost purred with contentment, as she watched the now embarrassed Damien reaching for his clothes and pulling them on quickly, telling her they were crazy to do what they had done! Simona jumped up from the bed and standing naked in front of him, she reached up to stroke his face.

"But, James, my darling, it was wonderful and we've done nothing wrong. My father likes you, *really* likes you, so he will be fine when I tell him I love you and want to marry you."

"Whaaat? No, you can't tell him! I mean, no, not yet." Damien was running on empty, his reasoning shot to pieces by the shock of what Simona had just said and the double-dose climax he'd experienced a short while ago. He had to think, quick!

As Simona pulled back, he took her hands and kissed her fingertips. "My darling, let's not tell him just yet. We need to do this right. Besides, it would be more fun to wait and enjoy the secrecy for a little bit longer." It was the best excuse he could think of, that would come anywhere close to satisfying Simona sufficiently to keep her quiet.

Simona smiled and kissed him again, "You are so right, my darling, it would be fun to keep us a secret. Just think, I can squeeze and touch your cock anytime I please and you won't be able to say or do anything about it!" The playful Simona was already fantasising about the fun involved in keeping their love affair secret, knowing she could exert her feminine power to tease him whenever she pleased. The thought of that alone turned her on, besides knowing that she still had a good stash of the white powder she'd slipped into James' drink earlier. Simona almost purred again, as she imagined the fun she would have using it.

Straightening his clothes and flattening his ruffled hair with some water, Damien checked the coast was clear before the two of them left her quarters to walk across to the main house. Simona had already planned the perfect alibi should they be questioned about James' absence; she would just say she had needed his help to reorganise her closet, having decided to clear out some of her old things.

In fact, Simona had no intention of explaining anything, knowing no-one would dare to question her, but she wanted to protect James, whilst enjoying more private time with him. Now, sitting at the table, which was still enjoying the last of the sun, she asked James to instruct Cook to bring the food they should have had for lunch. She was ravenous and could eat both lunch and whatever Cook was planning for dinner.

Damien felt immense guilt as he walked down to the kitchens to see Eliza. Nearing the main room, he could hear voices, which meant Armand was with her. Damn! Damien had to remain calm and not appear flustered in any way. If they questioned his damp hair, he would say that Simona pulled him into the pool, after asking him to help her out of the deep end and that he'd had to go and change, then she'd suddenly decided to clear out her closet! This was crazy, how many lies did he have to tell, how difficult a web was he weaving. *Oh, my god, Inga, I need you, I need our safe life back!* Damien's thoughts overtook his senses for a fleeting moment, until Eliza's voice snapped him back to reality.

"James, there you are. Why did you and Simona not have lunch?"

Damn, he'd not prepared an excuse for missing the lunch!

"Oh, Simona changed her mind, Cook. She went to lie down and must have fallen asleep. I just spoke to her though and she wants her lunch now please, on the terrace. I can take it through for you if you like?"

Damien was being super helpful, hoping that Eliza wouldn't notice his slightly damp hair, but she was no fool and had spotted it the moment he'd walked into her kitchen, as had Armand.

"Boy, you can't fool a kidder. I doubt she was sleeping alone and by your wet hair, I'm guessing something has happened between you two."

Eliza knew what Simona was like, as did Armand. Much as they both loved Simona, they also knew she teased and played with her father's men. Although, this was the first time they had suspected her to have taken one of them to her bed. At least, that had been their assumption when they couldn't find the pair of them earlier, but they liked James a lot, he was different to the other men who lusted after their precious Simona, so they felt okay with him having spent time alone with her.

"Watch your step, my boy. You know if you break her heart, her father will cut yours out and eat it!"

Eliza's comment was backed up by Armand. "Yes, James, my boy, watch yourself with that one, she's a handful!"

Damien's face reddened as he realised they'd been found out, but not before thanking his lucky stars that Eliza and Armand hadn't found them in the act earlier; he would definitely be a dead man if they had seen what he'd just done to their precious Simona. More to the point, what she had done to him too; the bite mark on his shoulder was still painful and red-raw.

"I'll be careful, Cook. She sure is a handful." James nodded at the gardener as he winked back at him and Cook shook her head, knowing there was trouble ahead for the young lovers.

Although, Damien was actually ten years older than Simona, he was very fit and his body easily compared to that of a man many years younger. Damien was ripped and very handsome, so Eliza and Armand could understand Simona's attraction to him.

Taking the tray, Damien walked back out to the terrace, knowing they would not be disturbed again. The

60

guard on the gate had already switched over and would be at his post all night. The gatehouse had its own toilet and kitchenette, so once the guard's evening meal was taken down to him, unless there was an emergency, he would not normally come back up to the house until the morning changeover took place. The tradition was, the guards ate dinner and lunch in the gatehouse but were invited to join the house-staff for breakfast.

Simona and Damien ate their meal and at Simona's suggestion, he opened a bottle of champagne, wondering how the hell he could get himself out of this mess. Simona was oblivious to the turmoil going on inside Damien's head as she settled back in the chair. Such potent, drug-induced sex had made her hungry and she soon ate most of the salad, main meal and fabulous dessert that Cook had sent up with James.

Feeling the same hunger, Damien was thankful of the generous plate that Cook had prepared for him too, but her words were ringing in his ears and he knew he had to tread carefully. Standing up to take the tray back to the kitchen, Damien told Simona he would only be a few minutes.

Feeling naughty and knowing their time alone was limited, the moment his back was turned, Simona poured a sachet of white powder into the champagne bottle; she needed to have James again before the night was out and she wanted him to make love to her in the water. Knowing Cook and the gardener could not see the pool from their rooms in the big house, Simona refilled both glasses with the drug-laced champagne and took a large drink while she waited for James to return.

Damien thanked Cook and bid the pair good evening, saying he would see them in the morning. Eliza and Armand would soon be retiring for the evening themselves, their own secret romance very much on their minds. The two of them had been carrying-on together for years, unbeknown to Simona, the Don, or his entourage. Skilled at deception over so many years, they were old hands, but they suspected James was like a rampant young buck and they feared for his safety, worried that his deception skills were not as polished as their own. Little did they know his true identity and just how skilled at deception James already was.

Damien returned to Simona, picking up his refreshed glass as he sat down, then sipping the bubbly liquid, thinking how this was not such a bad job after all. It could be a lot worse.

What? Are you mad? What are you thinking man, this is not a game!

Common sense slapped him in the face as he couldn't believe the thought that had just run through his mind. Brushing it aside, Damien supposed it was the comfortable closeness of Cook and the gardener which had lulled him into a false sense of security. As the next hour passed, Simona began asking James about his life. Keen to avoid any suspicion of foul play, Damien said he had been married before, but was now divorced. He boosted his lies by saying he had never had children and so divorce had been a relief, particularly as they were so young; he described it as a college romance.

Back on track with his official storyline, Damien relaxed, comfortable in the knowledge that he knew this storyline well. Taking another drink, he relaxed a little more and began feeling very comfortable with Simona; she really was a beautiful and entertaining woman, there was no hiding that fact.

Simona waited until they had finished the champagne before suggesting they skinny-dip in the pool. By this time, Damien was unknowingly under the influence of the white powder once again and going along with every one of her wishes. He stripped poolside and dived into the tepid water. He surfaced to watch carefully as Simona slipped the fine straps of her dress from her shoulders, allowing the beautiful silky fabric to fall to the ground. Having been wearing only the dress, Simona now stood completely naked, framed by the setting sun and the beautiful burnt orange sky. There was a hint of pink edging the few strands of cloud that were behind Simona as she stood in front of Damien, who was revelling in his admiration of her beautiful nakedness, whilst the softening light of the sunset bathed her skin with its warm tones. Damien encouraged her to join him in the water. Stepping towards the edge, she lowered herself in gracefully, gasping slightly at its coolness after the warmth of the evening air temperature and as her skin reacted to the water, her nipples hardened completely. Damien watched, cheekily enjoying her body's reaction, as his cock began to harden and he swam towards Simona. Taking her into his arms, he kissed her passionately. The two of them turned and swam away from each other, playing about as they splashed one another and laughing as the other tried to splash harder, before coming together again and, as was inevitable, completing their trio of sexual encounters. Simona's legs wrapped around Damien's hips as she rode his erect cock for the third time that day. The drugs had taken hold of them both, passion and lust, theirs for the night and unrelenting, they would find themselves awakening in the early hours to weak bodies and feeling hungry as hell, both for food and each other.

Chapter 7

Regrets

Damien could not believe what had happened to him again last evening, Simona's sexual appetite was insatiable and he had wanted to fuck her more times than he had ever done before in one night. This morning though, he was again full of regret at having betrayed Inga and he knew he could never tell her because understandably, she would never forgive him. Knowing that he must, Damien wondered if and how, he would live with his guilt forever. More to the point, how could he stop it happening again before the raid was complete? He felt sure that no matter whether the Don was here or not, Simona would find a way to have him again. His head was pounding and despite the pills he had taken on waking, Damien could not shake it off. The Don's plans had changed and he was now due back in four hours, so Damien had to pull himself together, and fast. Checking the car over, Damien was surprised when he heard Simona's voice.

"James, would you run me into town please? I need to collect a dress I ordered last week. I'll just change my shoes and be back in five minutes. Can you get the car ready?" There wasn't an optional answer to Simona's question. Damien knew he had to comply. Armand was close by and would have heard Simona's request.

"Sure, I'll just finish checking it over, be right with you." Damien was worried, this was not in his plan for today. He needed to ensure he was here when the Don arrived. "We will have to be quick though, your father will want to see me here when he returns."

"Oh, that's fine, James, I know he will, but it'll only take us a couple of hours," Simona reassured him, also being aware of the gardener's presence and not knowing that Armand was fully aware of her liaison with James the previous evening.

Sure enough, five minutes later, Simona was jumping into the front seat. Damien took his place at the wheel and started up the engine, waving to Armand as he drove them down towards the big gates. Pausing to inform the guard where he was taking Simona, Damien asked him to advise the Don where they were, should he return early. The guard was very familiar with Simona's demanding behaviour and signalled his understanding to James.

As the expensive car motored along the leafy roads of the hilly suburb, Simona remarked on how lovely the day was and how fabulous it was to have some private time with James, before her father returned home. Damien played along and agreed, placing his hand on her bare knee for effect. It was a mistake he would regret as they reached a secluded part of the suburb and Simona admitted that actually, she did not need to go into town and in fact, she wanted him to take the next left turn, which led into a very quiet, narrow road. Damien was worried, he had no clue where he was, or where they were going. When he asked her where they were headed, Simona reached across to touch his leg and said not to worry and that she just wanted to show him a secret place.

Oh, no! Damien worried that she was playing him and that no doubt she would want him sexually again. *Oh, Inga...* inside, Damien regretted his betrayal, yet he was excited by the thought of satisfying Simona again.

As they drew up outside a small, slightly dilapidated house, Simona said they could park around the side of the building, explaining that she knew the place well, having played there many times when she was a child. The house had been the home of her childhood nanny and despite being paid for by the Don, it had been left uncared for once Nanny had passed-on. The Don had not been able to bring himself to sell it, knowing that Simona loved spending time there, so it had just been left untouched and temporarily forgotten. Damien relaxed a little, realising it was quite private and therefore highly unlikely that they would be found. As the two of them stepped out of the open-top car, Damien commented on the heat, so Simona offered him some of her water. Unbeknown to Damien she had already laced the bottle with the tasteless white powder and being a blue bottle, Damien could not see there was anything wrong with it. He took a big gulp then said they'd best not be too long, reminding Simona about him needing to be back for her father. Damien hoped he could persuade Simona to just show him around, but he could see she was in a playful mood again. Unbeknown to him, she was already high from the drugged water she'd drunk in the car. Damien realised Simona was not going to give up without them having sex and so, to help allay his guilt and regret, he reminded himself of his boss' instruction to go with whatever she wanted, until the day they could bust the whole gang. Damien followed Simona as she took his hand and bending to miss the overgrown rose bush, she walked him around to the back of the house.

"Wow!" Damien saw the view from the garden of Nanny's house and understood why Simona had loved it there so much.

"Isn't it amazing, James?" Simona wanted James to love this place as much as she did, because her plan was to ask her father to revamp it and build a pool, so that she could have the house as her personal retreat.

"It sure is, Simona. You would never think this view was here from the front." James was so in awe of the view, he had forgotten about the expected sex and instead shared Simona's water again, as she showed him around.

As they ventured down the terraced garden, Simona showed James some of the hiding places she had played in as a child. Feeling nostalgic, she had also completely forgotten the white powder she'd added to her water bottle as she shared it with James. The heat of the day intensified, as did the effect of the drugs and as Simona turned to face James she asked an out-of-the-blue question, "Would you like to marry me and have babies with me, James?"

"Jeez Simona, where did that come from?" Damien's response did not please Simona and her face dropped.

Damien realised his mistake, but he was panicked by her unexpected and shocking question and his usual calmness seemed to have left him. Instead, he was worried, very worried as Simona turned towards him and in a disappointed voice said, "But I thought you loved me, James?"

"I do love you." Damien recovered remarkably well. "I just didn't expect that question from you, at least, not here, not today." Damien was back in control. Somehow, and he didn't know how, his voice and senses were now on super-alert. Pulling her into his arms, Damien said, "Of course I would marry you my darling, but I thought we were keeping this, us, a secret for now?" Damien hoped and prayed that Simona would revert to their original plan.

"Oh, sure, we can wait for a couple of weeks, but James, these last two days with you have been awesome.

We've had such great sex and I know it sounds crazy, but over the past weeks I've fallen for you, in a big way!" Simona reached up to kiss him before he could reply. As she did so, her hands moved down his back and reached around to his crotch; her voice was sensuous as she softly whispered, "Oh, my darling, make love to me now, if we can't tell anyone yet, we can at least consummate our promise to each other."

Simona was completely under the influence of the drug she had consumed and aside from making love to him, right here and now, marrying James was her only other desire. She was totally at one with her words and longing for him. Damien however, was not as far along the path of drug-induced craziness and he knew this was a really dangerous moment for him. Yet, he could not risk upsetting Simona when they were just days away from the raid, also knowing his boss would fire his arse if he screwed this up now. Carefully taking Simona's hand, he wavered momentarily and then kissed her fingers. Simona's pleasure increased and she told him she wanted him, desperately. Knowing the house was locked up and the garden overgrown, there was nowhere here for them to be intimate.

"The car!" Simona suggested gleefully.

Damien's eyebrows raised; he never would have thought Simona would be up for sex in a car. But he didn't know about the drugged water she had been drinking, or that he too was now being affected by it. Walking back up towards the house, Simona lead the way and, as she climbed the steps up the terraced garden, Damien watched her thighs and butt. Man, she was one sexy woman and his hands could barely resist reaching out to touch her inner thighs. The micro dress she was wearing had revealed her panties with every step and Damien was growing harder by the second. By the time they'd reached the car, the drug was taking full effect and he was feeling just as sexy and turned on, as Simona looked. The roof of the convertible was already down and it was as if the car were beckoning to them. Turning to kiss James, Simona then slipped off her panties and gave them to him, before stepping into the back-seat area of the car. The legroom was enormous, meaning there was plenty of room for them to fool around. Turning back to face James, Simona grinned at him as he pushed her panties into his pocket before unzipping his fly. She knew the risk of them being seen was slightly raised by being at the side of the house, despite the rose-covered railings, which offered a little privacy. But, she was totally uncaring about who might walk past, all caution having been thrown to the wind in her drug-induced sexiness. Simona desperately wanted to feel James inside her again. She knew that keeping their secret was going to be difficult and that she would probably not have him again until they had told her father of their plans. Damien stepped into the car and turned around as Simona watched his hands push down his shorts, revealing his already urgent want for her. Lowering himself onto the back seat, Damien invited Simona to sit astride him; she was ready and eager to please. Having planned this moment when dressing that morning, her chosen dress had buttons at the front and she had already begun undoing them to expose her pert, firm breasts. Damien looked at her and could no longer resist touching them, lifting her up so he could suck on her nipples, Simona gasped with pleasure, telling James she wanted him, needed him and was now going to have him as she sat down firmly on his hard cock, groaning as it reached deep inside her. Damien's head felt like it would explode, his mind was overtaken with desire as his lust grew and he thrust up into Simona's hot, wanting wetness, again and again. As they both reached the point of no return, voices could be heard, a man and a woman, slightly distant, but obviously coming their way. But, there was no way of stopping, Damien's last thrust caused his cock to shoot his hot load up into Simona, just as her body clenched onto him, unable to let go as she climaxed multiple times. This time their bodies were completely in tune and Damien's sperm made its way into Simona's welcoming belly. As their climax ended, the two of them, soaked with sweat, peeled themselves apart and laughing, quickly redressed, now anxious not to be caught in the act. As they stood up, Simona stepped towards James and kissed him again. He kissed her back, exploring her mouth with his tongue as he cupped her left breast, now safely hidden away beneath her dress. The drugs made him tremendously horny and he could have gone again, but the voices were getting closer so they should really control themselves, but feeling as he did, it didn't stop James slipping a hand under Simona's dress and pushing his fingers into her wetness again, rubbing and coaxing her until, just as the people walked past, she came again, this time sinking her teeth into James' shoulder to stop herself from crying out. Instead it was James who cried out, causing the two people to glance into the front of the property. Luckily, all they could see was two people embracing inside a very large open-top car, which they just took at face value and ignored as they continued walking.

Damien was sure Simona had broken his skin with her bite, but the two of them were so drunk on the effects of the drugs, that neither cared nor worried. Damien needed water and finished the remainder of the bottle before Simona could stop him. The two of them walked around to the back of the house and, finding a patch of grass where they could enjoy the view, they laid down and soon fell asleep on the sunny terrace, their after-sex exhaustion and the heat negating second-time sexual urges.

As Damien awoke to a setting sun, he panicked at the thought of the Don having already arrived home and he vigorously shook Simona to wake her. "Simona, wake up, we are in big trouble, your father will be home already. We've slept all afternoon!" Damien was very worried now, instantly feeling sober, knowing he was also now risking the whole operation. "Come on, we need to get back." Simona was awake and reluctant to break their afternoon of pure wanton pleasure.

"Oh James, do we have to go back? Can't we just stay here and enjoy the sunset?" Simona looked at him with puppy-dog eyes as she straightened her hair and brushed grass from her shoulders.

"We should really go back, Simona, let's not make your father angry, eh?" Damien was coaxing, but a sense of urgency was overcoming him. They really had to get back. "Come on, let's go." As he stood up, he held out a hand to Simona to help her to her feet.

Whilst Simona knew they had to go, she enjoyed teasing and toying with James and didn't make the journey home any easier on him. She was convinced she had found the man of her dreams and the sooner she could tell her father about her love for James, the better.

Damien however, was sobering by the minute and once again, his regret overwhelmed him as he thought of Inga and his betrayal of their love. Right at that moment, Damien was ready to throw in the towel on the job and walk away, but he knew that was impossible; he had to complete this mission, so instead he swore to himself that never again would he go undercover. Damien knew he needed to change what he did for a living if he was going to save his marriage.

As they pulled up to the gates, the guard informed 'James' that the Don was home. The lights in the house were all on. Damien's heart sank as he anticipated the hostile welcome he expected from the Don. Damn, he might just have blown the whole deal. Damien was thinking hard about how to manage the situation as they pulled up outside, whilst Simona had fallen silent. Both of them had now recovered from the effect of the drugs, as they slid out of the car and walked inside the house.

Chapter 8

The Boss and James

As the two of them entered the house, the Don's voice could be heard bawling out one of his men. Damien's heart sank, the Don's mood sounded dark and he expected much of the same treatment, after having driven Simona home much later than expected. The doors to the Don's office were wrenched open and he stormed out, obviously angered by the incompetence of Dino, the man he had been bawling out. But, no sooner had he laid eyes on Simona, his mood immediately softened and his face smiled at the two of them.

"Simona, my darling, how wonderful you look!" The Don hugged his daughter, who behaved like a child welcoming a long-lost father, as she hugged him back.

"Father, it's so good to see you! We have missed you, haven't we, James?"

Simona glanced towards Damien as he nodded and smiled back, before replying, "We sure have. Welcome back, sir."

The Don was not a foolish or unobservant man and he could see a sparkle in his daughter's eyes as she glanced across to his new man. He followed her gaze and held out a hand to Damien. "James, my boy, I can see you've been taking good care of my daughter, thank you!" Damien was shocked at the casual friendliness the Don portrayed as they shook hands.

"You're more than welcome, sir, it was my pleasure. I just hope I did as good a job as Leon." Damien didn't know what else to say, whilst Simona stifled a giggle, one not missed by the Don, as he invited James to join him in his study, leaving Simona to return to her rooms and refresh herself for supper. Pointing to the sofas beside the terrace doors, the Don instructed one of his men to bring them coffee and told the others to leave the room. The men were used to being ordered around, but all were intrigued by this familiarity with the new guy, James.

"James, my boy, sit down." The Don sat opposite Damien, making him feel even more uncomfortable and worried. "I see my Simona has a soft spot for you." As Damien began to protest, the Don waved him down. "It's okay James, I'm fine with it. I like you and if Simona is happy and trusts you, then so do I." As Damien breathed a little easier, the Don continued, "All I will say is, don't mess her around and don't make her cry." Damien gulped, knowing the undertone of that comment. "Now, tell me a bit more about yourself, because if I know my daughter well enough, I can see she really does like you a lot, so I need to know more about you."

The Don relaxed, whilst Damien felt evermore tense, as he imagined the Don being his real father-in-law and waving a gun around every time 'James' upset his daughter. Damien knew he had to tread very carefully and appear genuine, to retain the Don's trust. With only the storyline his bosses had given him, Damien weaved the little web of lies about his life as James, before quickly moving on to again speak about Simona, stating the obvious, of how beautiful she was and adding how he had become incredibly fond of her. The Don laughed several times throughout their conversation. He did like this young man and thought his daughter had made a good choice in him. James seemed like a real family man, just the kind of guy the Don wanted for his headstrong daughter.

Of course, only Damien knew how wrong the Don was on that point, proven by his own seemingly easy ability to betray his beautiful Inga. One thing Damien did now realise though, was that he had to be very careful not to give away any details of his real life. Inga would be in danger if the Don knew of her existence. Damien was normally highly skilled at working undercover, but this job was testing every ounce of his being and awareness. It was imperative he move the topic back to business and hoped that this newfound favour with the Don would mean his role in the upcoming delivery would be one which gave him access to the exact information his bosses were waiting on. Maybe this encounter with Simona could be more helpful than he had previously imagined. Damien considered how brave he could be with the Don and decided to broach the subject of dating his daughter.

Unaware of the sexual encounters Simona and James had already enjoyed, the Don respected James for asking permission to date Simona and gave his valuable agreement, reminding him again, not to mess her around, or to make her cry. A promise no man could reasonably agree to, which the Don knew only too well himself, however, he also knew that if he threatened James a little, the man would do his utmost to make Simona happy. This was all the Don wanted for his beloved daughter, as he again shook James' hand before turning the discussion to business.

Damien left the room two hours later with all of the information he needed. He was relieved that the main part of his job was done. The moment he could relay that information to his bosses, he would. Meanwhile, he had to play along with the role of being Simona's new boyfriend. At least, now the cat was out of the bag, he could relax a little and, provided Simona didn't want to ask her father if she could marry James within the next week, he was home and dry!

Damien made his way to the kitchens and smiled at Eliza, relieved that he could now tell her and Armand of the Don's approval for him to date Simona whilst also seeking their discretion over what had happened in the past few days. Eliza was thrilled, as both she and Armand liked James very much. They'd already decided that he seemed like a decent chap and a good choice for the little girl who had grown-up to become their beautiful Simona. Both of them had been aware of the bisexual tendencies Simona had felt and wondered if that would continue, or if, having now settled on James, that meant she had finished experimenting with and exploring her sexual orientation. Only time would tell on that count.

Simona entered her father's study to inform him that dinner was about to be served and was delighted when he beckoned her to his knee. As she sat for the last time, the Don knew his little girl was truly now a grown woman and one he was about to allow another man to interact with. It was an important stage in both their lives and, as he told her of his conversation with James, Simona hugged her father and wept tears of joy, telling him she already loved James and hoped that his love for her would grow strong enough to want her for his wife. The Don laughed, his own love for his daughter expanding with her every loved-up giggle and expression of happiness at the thought of becoming James' wife.

That evening, as they sat for dinner, James was invited to join the Don and Simona. An event which would become a regular occurrence and one that Damien would also very much enjoy over the coming days. Despite the reason for his presence inside this family home, he was beginning to feel a strong affection for Simona, not love of course, but definitely something more than it should be. On these occasions, Inga was forgotten and Damien was enveloped by the moment, the ambience, Simona's obvious affection for him and the welcome friendliness of the Don.

Thankfully, there had been no more sexual encounters for Damien to worry about, but something emotional was growing within him and that was beginning to worry him. He could not wait for the big delivery day to arrive, so he could escape this dangerously welcoming family empire.

Inga had not seen Damien for almost three weeks now and was almost beside herself with worry about what he was involved with this time. It was true that Damien's bosses kept her informed of his safety, but that was all, she was expected to just get on with her life in between the absences and that was becoming increasingly difficult for her. Inga knew this job was a big deal and so she was being patient, but she also felt like she was nearing the end of being able to cope with Damien's job. When he came home, she had to talk to him, she really wanted, no, *needed* him to change his job.

Inga desperately wanted Damien to stop working undercover and take the expected promotion of managing his own team of spooks, rather than participating in the frontline activities himself. There had been something very disconcerting about this job; Inga could almost feel that something about it was very different than before. Her senses were on full alert. The danger was increasing and despite the reassurances from Damien's bosses, instinctively, Inga knew that something was very wrong and she was afraid for husband's safety.

Since being a child, Inga had developed a kind of sixth sense and in all the years she had been with Damien, she often knew when he was in mortal danger, but this was different. The danger was not about death, but it was all-consuming and she was convinced that someone else was involved. The thought broke her heart, but she could not share it with any of her friends, having been sworn to secrecy over all matters related to Damien's work. Whilst her heart silently broke, Inga made up her mind, this time things really did have to change, either that, or their life together would have to end. There was no going back, of that Inga was becoming ever more certain.

Feeling particularly sad, Inga knew she needed a pick-me-up and so she called Kate. Knowing that Pete was away again, Inga asked Kate if she was free for dinner the next evening. Thrilled to hear from Inga, Kate admitted that she too was feeling a little fed up with being home alone, whilst Pete was away working, so the two friends agreed to meet up at Antoine's. The timing worked out quite well, because their usual weekly gathering with the girls had been put on the back burner for a couple of weeks – mainly due to holidays and work commitments – which meant a night out at Antoine's was just what the doctor ordered, for both women.

As they walked through the door, Antoine spotted the girls and waving madly at them, he made his way across the room, welcoming and ushering them in enthusiastically. Antoine had missed seeing the girls and with Pete away too, he had felt compelled to totally focus on his business, which in truth, was always busy and in need of his attention.

"It's so lovely to see you, Kate. I've missed you and your friends!" Antoine kissed Kate on both cheeks and then did the same to Inga, much to her delight.

"Oh, Antoine, I know what you mean, it seems such an age since we last came in. Everyone has been so busy, what with work and holidays. We've just not had a chance to get together." Thanking Antoine as he offered his best available table, Kate continued, "Which is why Inga and I thought that seeing as Damien and Pete are both away, we would pop in for something to eat and say hello to our favourite restaurateur!" Kate winked and grinned at Antoine, who appreciated the gesture, whilst also empathising with Kate.

"I have to admit, I've missed seeing Pete too, he seems to be away a lot at the moment." Pete really was Antoine's best mate and the two of them saw each other regularly. Pete liked to pop in and chat to Antoine during his food-prep time, sometimes giving a hand and working together on recipes previously enjoyed in Antoine's family home. The two of them were like brothers and worked well together, enjoying reminiscing over old times and catching up on family news.

As the girls settled down, Antoine took their orders himself. The friends slipped into an easy familiarity, discussing the merits of Pete's work taking him away from home so much. Inga was able to totally understand that longing, what with Damien's current home vs. work status, especially with the home status being mainly absent.

Inga and Kate thoroughly enjoyed their evening together, the food was great, as it always was at Antoine's and the ambience met their needs. The end result was that both women felt a little better as the evening wore on. Yet Inga still had a deep sense of foreboding, there was definitely something amiss, she sensed it, but knew she could not share it. A fact that was driving her crazy.

Back at the Don's house, Damien was lying in bed, having been offered a room to stay overnight, following a very boozy dinner and evening. Inga was on his mind and he hated the fact that he could not just go home to see her and hold her, he needed to tell her that he loved her. *He did love her, didn't he?* Yes, of course he did, admonishing himself for even thinking such a doubtful thought. But, it was his growing feelings for Simona which were now blurring his mind. *Damn!* He had to stay focussed and keep his mind on the job. As the hours ticked by, Damien felt unable to sleep, such was his torment. He absolutely knew he had to get out of this place before he did something there truly was no coming back from. It was the early hours of the following morning before Damien finally fell asleep, exhausted by the worry and stress he was now living under, during his every waking hour.

A loud knock on the door awoke Damien. It was Simona, bringing him coffee. Oh, my God, he saw the time. Damien was an hour later rising than normal and didn't want to be late to the Don's breakfast meeting with the men. The Don was usually pretty tough on anyone who arrived late and today was a big one. Immediately jumping out of bed, Damien forgot he was totally naked, much to Simona's amusement, as she quickened her pace across the room towards him whilst reaching out to touch every part of him that she so desired.

"Well, good morning James, my darling, I can see you're as pleased to see me as I am to see you!" Simona winked and giggled as she took the fullness of his usual morning erection into her hands. Damien had to resist without upsetting her and kissed her briefly, before making his excuses to retrieve his now even harder cock, which, having momentarily enjoyed the warmth of Simona's hands, clearly wanted more.

Damien held her hands in his as he spoke. "I have to go down for the breakfast meeting, but thank you for bringing me coffee, although I don't think I can drink it right now." As he saw her smile fade a little, Damien added a hasty, "I could take it with me though." This seemed to satisfy Simona, as she relented and smiling back at him, said she would see him later.

Today was the penultimate day before the shipment of drugs and guns was due to arrive. The mood at the Don's morning meeting was extremely serious, with only those present who needed to be in the know, each confirming their role in the final arrangements. Damien was fully alert and absorbing every detail, ready for relaying back to his real bosses later that day. Everything had been planned to the smallest detail, both with the Don's men and the law enforcement teams, who were ready and waiting to pounce; making this the biggest combined bust that they hoped to successfully achieve. The deal was worth an obscene amount of money, which the Don was planning to use to fund his daughter's whole future, as well as his own retirement; having decided it was time to hand over the reins to someone else.

Damien knew this was a huge deal for the Don, but he also hoped it would be successful enough for his own upcoming promotion, followed by a future move into the ranks of senior management. If he could pull that off, it meant he would no longer be on the frontline and could not be tempted by the next 'Simona'.

Still totally unaware of the drugs Simona had used on him, in his raw state of mind, Damien was crucifying himself over his betrayal of Inga and their marriage. And yet, there was no denying it, his attraction to Simona was there and growing and he hated himself for feeling it. Aside from the drugs, the memory of their great sex had burned into his mind and the luxurious life he could potentially have, if he were to marry Simona, was a far cry from his suburban life with Inga.

Inga, whom he had truly loved with all his heart and yet whom, in that very moment, seemed to become increasingly distant in his thinking, as thoughts of making love with Simona rushed in.

What the hell was he doing? Oh, my God, was his mind seriously considering a life with Simona? Without Inga? Checking himself, Damien knew he was totally screwed up, this was the most crucial operation that he had ever been involved in, but he hadn't bargained on falling for anyone, let alone the Don's daughter, or becoming ever closer to the Don himself — the man he was working to ensure would be going to jail for the next twenty to thirty years — and whose daughter would want to kill him, should his true identity and involvement ever be revealed. What had he gotten himself into?

Damien knew the story he was to follow, at the moment the raid took place, which had been designed to throw off the scent of his involvement, but now, with all that had happened, escaping Simona's clutches was going to be far from easy. The plan was for him to appear to take a bullet, whilst protecting the Don, that way there would be no repercussions. Word would be released that he had died following the shooting, which would let him off the mafia hook. The theory was there, but Damien hadn't bargained on Simona, or him having any feelings for her, or her father.

Fighting his own moral battle, with the devil on one shoulder and the good angel on the other, Damien wondered what the hell he was going to do. Whilst he knew he was meant to return to his real life and let go of the sexy Simona, her marvellous home and the promised, exciting, future life he could have with her. Confusion reigned. The drugs and Simona had really screwed with Damien's head and he was in a total quandary over what to do about her and his life with Inga.

Chapter 9

Judgement Day

The big day had finally arrived and as they waited for the delivery of merchandise to arrive, tensions began to mount. Each man privately reflected on this moment, knowing it was the Don's last deal and worth millions. The payoff was guaranteed to be even more generous than usual, if everything went according to plan. Still totally unaware of who James really was though, or what his betrayal would mean for them all, the men waited, anxious, but excited, at the prospect of the handsome payoff the Don had promised them. Their hearts were already pounding with anticipation and fear of anything going wrong. All of their lives and futures depended on this exchange running like clockwork. Nobody dared screw up.

The location for the exchange was less discreet than one might expect, the idea being that normal activity would raise less suspicion. That said, the exchange was due to happen during the hours of dusk, with every possible effort to remain anonymous having been considered. Unusually, but not unexpected given the circumstances, the Don was overseeing this high value exchange himself, trusting no-one and feeling concerned about their risk of failing if a wrong word was spoken, or unexpected movement made.

The docks were always busy with container arrivals and the offloading from and onto trucks. This meant their expected containers should not raise any suspicions. Having been received and logged, the containers were to be sent for customs clearance, which was the point at which they would intercept. The plan being to swap the already loaded container trucks, with exact replicas. Every detail, down to the codes stamped on the side of the replicas, had been considered and planned for.

Dino, Mack and Jake were the Don's chosen drivers and the men he trusted the most. Having been well-briefed, they knew their routes inside out and were grateful to be considered the most trustworthy. Not that any of the Don's men would ever consider crossing him, for they all knew, without any doubt, that any betrayal would absolutely lead to a life of fear, always looking over their shoulder, waiting for the knife or bullet that would inevitably kill them.

As patience waned, tension caused adrenaline to kick in with most of the Don's men; they could feel their hearts beating and palms sweating as they waited, knowing they were considered the best, but also knowing they were only human and a bullet would kill them easily enough if they messed up. Dino in particular, was appreciative of the regained respect he now had, following the recent bawling-out he'd received from his boss and was thankful to the Don for trusting him again. Dino's determination was strong, in spite of the adrenaline.

The driver's brief was to zigzag across the country to three separate destinations, stay in their cabs overnight, before then moving on to a central location the following day and arriving two hours apart; the trucks would then be offloaded into a warehouse owned by the Don. The detours would ensure everything seemed totally innocent to any watchful eye.

Monies were to be paid by electronic transfer, speeding away to multiple offshore banks, the moment the first exchange was made. The Don was known and trusted, but with the large sums involved, the seller's representatives would be close by, waiting for the confirmation of funds received, before they allowed the trucks to be driven away; their own vehicles already blocking the trucks from moving forward.

Unbeknown to any of them, the MI5 sting had been well-prepared, with quayside dock-workers in their locality, substituted by armed police and Special Forces. Confident that their numbers would completely overwhelm the Don's men, as well as the seller and his associates, Mike Day was convinced of a successful outcome and was unwavering in his grit and determination to bring down the Don, the seller and all of the men involved.

Having been reassigned as the Don's personal driver, Damien's MI5 instructions were to ensure the Don's car was also blocking the exit. Damien had agreed with Mike that the least suspicious method of doing that, would be for the car to drop the Don off, reverse back enough to block the exit, but then for the car to not restart when Damien turned the key in the ignition. The result of a quick rewiring job inside the car and a skill Damien had perfected over the years.

Damien was more tense than usual as his own heart and head were conflicted by loyalties to his MI5 team and Simona's father. Whilst Damien knew the Don would of course be arrested, he wanted him to be captured unhurt, so that Simona could at least visit him in prison.

The armed police and Special Forces teams closed in around the gang, this was everyday work to them. However, the men who made-up the Don's gang, were beginning to feel frustrated at the delay caused by his car, which was now blocking the route out for all of their vehicles. As Damien tried to start the car again, the men grew anxious and jumpy, but by the time their suspicions were raised enough for them to run, they were also surrounded. Realising it was a raid, a voracious gun-battle started as the men dived for cover behind cars, piles of pallets and the nearest containers. As the relentless shooting continued, it was apparent that they were surrounded and yet, still they fought, never wanting to give up, knowing life in prison was the only out for them if they were captured. Inevitably, panic grew amongst the men and anger took over as one by one, their number reduced. Some were caught in the gangster crossfire, whilst others were taken down by the Special Forces team the moment their guns were fired and heads were raised. There was no messing about, it was shoot to kill on both sides, but even as their numbers dwindled, both gang members continued firing. Anger and fear hung in the air like a black cloud, as the smell of gunsmoke wafted across the docks and the loud bangs became a thud, as they reached a human target. The Don had been sheltering behind a car and as the bullets whizzed past him, he shouted out to James for help. Having taken a gunshot wound to his chest, the Don was bleeding profusely. Damien managed to work around to where the Don now lay and grabbing hold of him, hauled him behind the nearest car. Mike Day had informed all official shooters of Damien's presence and instructed that he was to be protected and not shot at.

Having seen a different side to the Don during recent weeks and finding him almost charming at times, Damien had actually grown to like the old man. No way did he want the Don to end up dead, yet Damien knew Simona's father must be tried for the crimes he had committed, including this one. So, whilst protecting the Don and as previously agreed with his own boss, Damien appeared to take a bullet in his thigh. Shouting out in pain, he gripped his leg, crushing the fake blood capsules strapped under his trousers, bursting them, encouraging the red dye to seep into the fabric. Damien looked around at the Don, who had now slumped to the floor, his own blood seeping profusely from a damaged artery and he called out towards the Don, "I'm hit, goddammit, how did this happen? Who knew about this except us?" Damien was playing his part perfectly but was also now extremely worried for the life of Simona's father. Dragging himself closer to the old man, Damien pressed hard on his chest wound, to help stem the bleed.

The Don looked into his eyes and thanked him, adding, "James my boy, if I don't make it, take care of Simona for me." The colour drained from his face as he slumped unconscious against Damien.

Ten minutes later, the battle was won and those of the Don's men who were still alive, were rounded up, along with the seller and his associates. Damien had already slumped into 'unconscious mode' which was purely for the benefit of the Don's men, who were all now laid out on the ground, handcuffed and only able to watch, as both their boss and James were loaded into waiting ambulances. Several of the Don's men were dead and whilst the MI5 raid was successful in taking such a large haul of drugs and guns off the street, as well as capturing the Don, it had been a bad result for the other five gang members who didn't make it through the gun battle. One of the dead was Dino.

Damien had mixed feelings. The sense of relief that he could now return to his normal life, was confused by sadness at seeing the Don badly injured. Also, so many of the men he had come to know were now lying dead and Damien could not help but feel a sense of loss at the end result. As James, he would be announced as having died on arrival at the hospital, following uncontrollable arterial blood loss from the gunshot wound to his upper thigh and a second wound to his abdomen. Which would satisfy any curiosity and enable Damien to leave his undercover role behind.

Neither Simona, the Don, nor his men would ever see 'James' again. At least, that was the plan.

The hospital staff were under strict instructions not to let anyone visit the Don, unless cleared by Mike Day. Armed guards were already in place and watched the Don at all times, including whilst he was in the emergency room, operating theatre and the private side-room which had been allocated to him.

Meanwhile, MI5 agents went to the house to inform Simona of her father's condition and fetch her to the hospital immediately. Mike Day needed to control her access to the Don, knowing she would not stay away once she knew of his condition. In his opinion, it was best they had her there, where they could watch and control her. But, Damien's boss had not accounted for Simona's insistence on seeing James' body, having also been told of his death. Simona was distraught and in shock at what had happened, but equally determined to say her own goodbyes to James because she really did love him and just had to see him.

Damien, having not had time to fully confess to Mike Day as to quite how deeply undercover he had really gone with Simona over the past week, was now quickly bringing his boss up to speed on the situation and receiving a verbal arse-kicking for his trouble. There was nothing for it though, they had to put that discussion to one side and find a way to throw Simona off the scent. Damien was taken down to the morgue and laid in a body bag, with strict instructions to lie perfectly still. The body bag was the best way they could show his body, without Simona realising he was actually still breathing. Having already been told she could only identify him through a glass window, Simona was angry, but accepted the restriction under the circumstances. In truth, Simona had expected to be arrested herself, just for the association of her relationships with both James and her father.

The morgue attendant had been replaced by one of Damien's own female colleagues and was now dressed in blue scrubs, as she calmly unzipped the bag enough to reveal James' blood-stained face. Simona broke down. Damien could hear her wracking sobs and his own stomach churned with every wretched, grief-stricken cry as he laid motionless in the body-bag, forced to listen to Simona's heart breaking. At no other time in his life had Damien felt so utterly bereft at himself and he decided there and then, that he would never go undercover again, even if his promotion was bounced. Damien never wanted to hurt another Simona. In his opinion, she didn't deserve this. It was her father who was bad, not her.

During the days that followed, Damien was debriefed and reprimanded for not being completely honest and open about the depth of his feelings for Simona *before* the day of the raid. But, as well as the reprimand, he was also recognised for bringing the job in. Never before had they successfully captured such a valuable haul of arms and drugs. The street-value alone was in the multi-millions bracket, but not only that, they had finally captured the head of the mafia family, who had always been a slippery character, forever escaping the clutches of the law, despite them knowing he was responsible for so many killings. But, because this time he was actually at the scene of the crime, they had him bang to rights and the Don's arrest was massive!

Damien was informed he *would* get his promotion and with immediate effect, thereby moving into a behind-the-scenes role of managing his own team of spooks. On the one hand, Damien was thrilled because he had wanted this promotion for so long, but he was also torn over the damage he had caused. It was true that he had told Simona he loved her, intending it to be a pretence, but he now realised that actually, he did have real feelings for her, even if they had been driven by pure lust.

Most importantly though, Damien also knew he just had to tell Inga the truth. Inga deserved that much and even though Damien knew for sure that she would not welcome his honesty over this one, he also knew that he could not spend a lifetime with her, with such a huge non-disclosure between them.

Obviously, disclosing the whole truth would destroy both Inga and their relationship, so Damien imagined a version of the truth with a kinder explanation. One which would *not* elaborate fully on the depth of his sexual encounters with Simona or his confused feelings for her. Instead, he would just admit to sleeping with her and claim it was for the sake of the job. *That way it was no worse than an affair, wasn't it?* Damien felt physically sick and didn't know what was worse, to confess to that or be totally truthful, knowing he would absolutely lose Inga. *Selfish, that's what you are man, fucking selfish!* Damien was cursing himself. This was a no-win situation for him and he knew it.

Inga was in the kitchen when she heard the key turn in the front door and Damien's voice calling out to her. Despite her senses having warned her of bad news, Inga was excited and thrilled that Damien was home and her happiness was undeniable as she rushed into his waiting arms. Damien hugged her to him tightly, before picking her up and swirling her around, then kissing her laughing mouth hard, crushing her lips with his. In that moment, there was no doubt in his mind that he still loved Inga and he convinced himself that returning to their normal life was what he really wanted. It was true that he really had missed her and again, mentally cursed himself for betraying her, but, he reasoned, he was just a man, a red-blooded male who had been swayed by Simona's sexual appetite for him, several times. The fact that had happened far too easily was not lost on him, but then of course, he was unaware that Simona had drugged him. Both to influence his attraction to her and improve his performance and stamina in the bedroom.

Unexpectedly, Inga pulled herself back from his embrace and stared into his eyes as she said, "I know something is wrong, Damien, but don't tell me what it is just yet, I want you to take me upstairs."

Damien's face gave away his guilt, but as his wife had requested, he lifted her into his arms and took her to their bedroom. The room smelled of her perfume and his wanting for her totally overwhelmed his senses as he gently set her down to stand in front of him. Momentarily, her eyes were searching his for answers, but she also didn't really want to ask the question that was toying with her mind and she certainly didn't want to know the answer, not until her animalistic instincts had been satisfied. Their sexual tension took over as they began undressing each other and soon they were pulling their clothes off frantically. Damien's cock was growing hard at the anticipation of entering Inga's warm softness, wanting her to welcome him completely. As she slipped off her panties, he sucked in his breath, totally in awe of her beauty, as his eyes travelled up and down her body, drinking in every part of her. *Was it love, or just lust?*

Damien didn't even consider that thought as he reached for her, his hands exploring her body as his kiss again crushed hers. They fell onto the bed together and his lips moved down to take her breasts into his mouth and sucking her nipples so hard that she cried out. Feeling turned-on so much that she felt ready to explode into a full orgasm the moment Damien entered her, Inga was crying out with pleasure whilst almost begging him to get inside her, "Now Damien… I want you now… Get in me… Please, get in me… " Damien needed no second asking, his fingers had already felt her wetness and he knew she was ready for him as he thrust up into her. On just the fifth thrust, they came together, his cock spurting hot sperm with every clench of Inga's orgasm as it gripped him, again and again. Their groans were combined, as their legs simultaneously weakened with every pulse of lust for each other and as the last thrust left them both satisfied, the love they both felt was theirs, had sown its seed in Inga's soft belly.

Rolling apart again, the two of them laid flat, just staring up at the ceiling, both panting as their passion and breathing began to steady.

It was Inga who spoke first. "Damien, I know something happened on this last job. But, I have thought about it a lot and decided that I really don't want to know the details. I just need to know if you still love me?"

Damien had tears in his eyes, knowing he didn't deserve this get-out-of-jail-free-card. Inga was one hell of a woman and he counted himself very lucky as he replied, "Inga, my darling, my love for you has never died." Pausing as Inga breathed a sigh of relief, Damien felt he had to confess a little, if only to ease his own conscience. "It is true that I have done things on this job that I never wanted to do. There are no excuses other than the fact that I was ordered and tested, and I failed, but my love…" Damien rolled onto his side to look at Inga and run his hand gently from her face to her soft belly, "I am back now and I love you, very much. I have won my promotion and will be given my own team. I even told them I never want to go undercover again!"

It was Inga's turn to roll towards Damien and she began to cry, burying herself into his arms, as he apologised to her, his voice softly repeating the words, "I'm so sorry my love," murmuring into her hair, as she wept against his chest. Damien told Inga again and again how much he loved her and said that this was the start of a new future for them both. Together. If she still wanted him?

Inga's tears masked relief as well as a sense of betrayal. She was no fool and it didn't take a rocket scientist to work out that Damien had obviously slept with another woman, but Inga also felt totally loved, as both their reactions on seeing each other had proven. Now, lying together and Damien telling her how much he loved her, Inga felt like they really could put the past behind them. The two of them pulled the duvet over themselves and stayed in bed for hours, as they talked, cried and laughed, promising each other to always be truthful, no matter what needed to be discussed or disclosed.

Being human, it was a promise that neither was sure the other could keep, but each hoped they could, for there had been a cleansing of conscience and a promise of willingness to always try to be honest with each other. Each knowing full well that their future depended on that honesty from now on.

Several hours later, the two of them, now hungry and in need of food, crawled out from under the duvet and made their way to the kitchen. Neither wanted to cook anything major and so they settled for toast and eggs, nice and easy, with some pre-grated cheese thrown in for extra bulk. Cooking naked was new to them both and felt a little bit naughty, but it was so sexy that they didn't care. Nobody could see them, so they enjoyed the freedom of touching and kissing whilst they prepared the food. The tabletop did beckon a few times, but they managed to resist each other until after they had eaten. But then dishes suddenly ended up on the floor as Damien swept them aside to take Inga again. As she lay back with her legs wrapped around him, Damien entered her, pushing in deep, pulling her towards him as he pushed in again and again, "Oh my God, Inga, you're so amazing." Inga lapped up every word as she held on with her legs, feeling her breasts bouncing with every thrust, as again, they came together, laughing at the naughtiness of the moment, but happy, so very happy. Thoughts of Simona were far from Damien's mind in that moment.

The following day was the start of the weekend and Damien had decided to take Inga out to their favourite restaurant. A special day of spoiling his wife was in order and he did not want to disappoint her; she could have everything she wanted, champagne, flowers, diamonds, anything. Damien loved her and wanted to make up for his appalling behaviour. But, all Inga wanted was him, them, together, excluding all others, just like the vows they had taken when they married.

Inga was happy again. Finally, her man was back and totally with her, of that she was sure. Damien loved her and that was all that mattered now.

Chapter 10

Unexpected News

Several weeks after Damien's return home, Inga suggested that as he hadn't seen their group of friends for a while, they should have a garden party and invite everyone. Agreeing enthusiastically, Damien admitted he was keen to get back into the throes of their normal married life and seeing friends again. Happy at Damien's reaction, Inga felt revitalised because she too wanted to get back to normal as much as Damien did.

"Perfect, I'll call round everyone and see if we can arrange something for two weeks on Saturday." Inga was excited and pleased to be planning something they would both enjoy. So, that very day, calls were made and as luck would have it, everyone was either already available, or said they would change plans to be there. They had all missed seeing Damien too and with an afternoon of good food on offer and lots of drinking, accompanied by their usual jokey banter, the gathering seemed like a perfect idea to them all. Not only that, everyone knew Inga was an amazing cook and that the food would be delicious. Kate was very happy to report that Pete would be back home from his latest contract by then, so he would also be able to join in the fun.

Those next two weeks saw Damien heavily involved at work, preparing case notes for the trial against Simona's father and his men. This meant the garden party arrangements had to be left for Inga to handle, not that she minded, she was very happy just getting back to normal and having Damien around so much more than before, which felt great for them both.

Two days before the party though, Inga awoke feeling quite sick and as she rushed out of bed to throw up in the bathroom, Damien waited anxiously outside the door, calling through to ask if she was okay. When Inga did emerge, she looked washed out. Damien hugged her, worrying what was wrong, whilst also feeling useless at being unable to do anything to help her. Inga groaned and pulled away from Damien to slump back into bed, now worrying herself about the food preparation she had planned for that day. It was not like her to be ill and she was really concerned that she had caught some kind of bug, which would mean they would most probably have to cancel the party because she didn't want to risk passing anything on to their friends.

Just as Damien was about to respond to her concerns, Inga flew out of bed again and ran back into the bathroom, throwing up the moment she reached the toilet. Damien was gutted at having to concede that they would likely have to postpone.

When Inga returned from the bathroom for the second time, he suggested calling Kate to see if she could pop over and keep Inga company. They both knew that this was really unfortunate timing because Damien absolutely had to be in the office for a run through of the trial papers, which had been planned for eleven o'clock that morning. Feeling torn between concern for his wife's well-being and a responsibility to attend such a crucial meeting, Damien realised he had no choice, he would have to go in. Inga understood. In truth, she was only too pleased to know this whole trial was almost over and she didn't want to delay anything. So, in true stoic style, Inga assured Damien she would be fine until Kate arrived, instructing her husband to hide a door key outside, so that Kate could let herself in. Damien felt bad at leaving Inga when she was feeling so unwell, but, knowing he had no choice, he kissed her and said he hoped she felt better soon, adding that he would call Kate from the car.

Thankfully, Kate wasn't busy and on hearing how ill Inga was, said she would be more than happy to pop over and help out. Damien thanked her, saying he'd call to check on them as soon as he could.

Thirty minutes later, having retrieved the door key from beneath the third flowerpot on the back garden decking, Kate turned the key in the lock and called out to Inga, only to hear her in the bathroom, throwing up the final remains of her stomach contents.

"Oh, my goodness, Inga, you poor thing, you really are not well, are you?" It was more of a statement than a question, but Kate was really concerned when she saw how white Inga's face looked.

Feeling totally drained, Inga thanked Kate for coming and said she just needed some water. Kate obliged, but before going to fetch a glass from the kitchen, she suggested that perhaps they should postpone the garden party, reassuring Inga that whilst everyone would be as disappointed as the both of them, their friends would also totally understand her dilemma. The thought of cancelling the party made Inga even more determined to shake off her feeling of sickness. As she pulled herself up in the bed and drank some water, she felt a little better. Dragging the wicker chair in the corner of the room across to the bed, Kate sat down and asked Inga if she thought it was food poisoning.

"No, I really don't think so Kate and there haven't been any bugs around. What do you suppose it could be?" Inga was desperate to identify the cause of this sudden sickness, so that she didn't have to cancel the party.

Kate was as puzzled as she was, but trying to cheer her friend up, she jokingly offered her explanation, "Well, if it's not food poisoning or a tummy bug, with Damien being home so much, it can only mean you're pregnant!" Chuckling at her off-the-cuff comment, Kate stopped when she saw Inga's mouth drop open.

"Pregnant?" Inga was shocked, then overwhelmingly hopeful, as realisation began to dawn and she quickly calculated the weeks since her last period. Inga looked down at her tummy.

Kate continued, having not seen Inga's smile, "Well, Damien has been away a while and presumably, you two have been at it like rabbits since he got back?" Smiling, having carefully phrased that question, Kate hoped that Inga and Damien had managed to patch up the marital issues which Inga had previously shared with Kate.

Thinking back, Inga remembered their love making on the day Damien came home and wondered if that explosive session had been the clincher and that finally, she might really be pregnant!

"Oh, my goodness, Kate, you could be right. Oh wow, how wonderful would that be!" Inga was now beaming with excitement as the colour began to return to her cheeks. Kate got up to hug her friend, hoping that a little miracle baby would be just what the relationship doctor ordered for Inga and Damien. The timing was perfect now that Damien's new job was on the horizon.

Both Inga and Kate let the thought of a new baby take over their conversation completely, until Kate suggested she pop to the chemist to get a pregnancy test kit. To which Inga beamed and nodded enthusiastically, "Oh, would you Kate? That would be awesome! Oh, my goodness, I can't believe it! Kate, this is such exciting news!" Inga was absolutely thrilled at the idea that she might really be pregnant, finally!

"Well, let's take a step back a minute, before we get too carried away and start ordering a pram." Kate laughed as she added, "Let me get the kit, you can do the test and then we'll know, one way or the other." Inga agreed, nodding happily, before diving off the bed and into the bathroom again. Kate called out she wouldn't be long and left Inga to her morning sickness.

Having rushed to the nearest chemist and now walking back to Inga and Damien's home with the kit tucked away in her bag, Kate's phone rang and Lowry's face appeared on the screen.

"Lowry! How are you doing?" Kate hadn't spoken to Lowry in a while and was very happy to hear from her oldest friend.

"Hey kiddo, I'm back in town tomorrow and I have some exciting news!" Lowry was clearly on cloud nine. "I've met a woman, well, she was flying in on the shuttle a few days ago and guess what, we just clicked. She lives miles away from me, but Kate, oh my goodness, she is so beautiful and sexy, and, well, she seems to totally have the hots for me. Although, I think that might be her hormones because she's pregnant and yes, before you say it, apparently, the father is no longer on the scene. Besides, she actually bats for my team too! Lucky me, eh? I really want you to meet her, so, can I bring her round tomorrow afternoon? Are you guys free?" Lowry had barely stopped for breath and took Kate's own breath away with the enthusiasm of her call.

Kate laughed as she told Lowry how absolutely thrilled she was for her and that yes, she would love to meet this wonder woman who seemed to have made Lowry the happiest woman on the planet. Then, remembering that she was due to be at Inga and Damien's party, she explained the dilemma to Lowry, whose mood then dropped like a stone. Kate quickly added, "Tell you what, leave it with me, I'll speak to Inga and see if we can add you guys to the invite. I'm sure it'll be fine, Inga knows you and is always happy to have extra people round."

Kate knew that Inga liked Lowry and felt sure it wouldn't be a problem to add two more to the guest list, if the party was still going ahead, but, politeness drove her caution and the concern that Lowry would be throwing this new lady-friend into the deep end, meeting so many friends at once. Lowry dismissed Kate's concerns, confident that it really wouldn't be a problem for her new girlfriend.

"Oh, that would be fab, Kate, totally fab. I mean, absolutely awesome!" Lowry was buzzing with so much excitement that Kate thought she might burst and told her so. The two friends laughed at the happiness of Lowry's news and mood then rang off, with promises to speak later.

Turning the key in the lock, Kate called out to Inga, who had subsequently moved from the bed to the shower and was just towel-drying her short hair; having also not peed whilst waiting excitedly for the pregnancy test kit to arrive. Inga felt as though her bladder were about to burst as she quickly took the package from Kate's hand and ran back into the bathroom.

Ten minutes later, both women were sat on the edge of the bed, watching closely as two pink parallel lines appeared on the plastic pee-stick.

"YES!" Inga was ecstatic and bounced across the room, sickness forgotten as she punched the air with a happiness that nothing could destroy. "Oh, my God, Kate, a baby, a baby, we're going to have a baby!" Kate was totally thrilled for Inga and hugged her friend, enjoying the delight that this wonderful news had brought.

"I can't wait to tell Damien! Oh, Kate, this is such marvellous news and just what we both need!" Inga was delirious with excitement, her emotions running riot and like many others, mistakenly imagining that having a baby would fix everything that had been broken between them recently.

Kate was excited for them, but with her own feet still firmly planted on the ground, she hoped beyond hope that this would indeed be the missing link for Damien and Inga. Hugging her friend again, she checked they were going ahead with the gathering of friends and felt utterly relieved when Inga replied with an excited, "Yes, Yes, Yes!"

As her elation settled to a calmer pace, Inga assured Kate that she felt much better now. So, the two women made their way down to the kitchen to begin preparing as much as they could for the garden party the next day. Whilst Inga had the whole of the following morning to finish preparations, just getting the table sorted out and marinating the meat was a massive help. Feeling very grateful for Kate being there, Inga told her so, more than once, to which Kate just laughed and said, "That's what friends do, isn't it, Inga? They help each other!" At which point, Kate remembered Lowry's call and told Inga about the new love interest Lowry had met on her last flight home. Not knowing many details, Kate just said that Lowry wanted to pop round to share the news with everyone and introduce them to her new friend. Inga was in the happiest of mindframes, still on a high from her baby news, so she was absolutely fine to include unexpected guests.

The two women chatted all day as they worked, completing the preparations by four o'clock and having stopped for a light snack. After which, Inga had felt much better, her stomach having returned to normal status. Until the morning at least. The news of her pregnancy had completely taken over Inga's mind and she could not wait to tell Damien. As the two women hugged and said their goodbyes, Kate wished Inga good luck in telling her husband the exciting news. Not that luck was needed, it was just something she said automatically, knowing the problems they'd had previously. Waving goodbye as she walked out the gate, Kate set off for home, calling Lowry on the way to let her know the invite was on.

Damien was tired, it had been a long day and the trial papers were a mission to get through, but it was done and they were ready. He was looking forward to going home to Inga when a call came through from the hospital. The Don had been re-admitted to hospital from the prison cell he had been held in following the shooting several weeks ago. This time, his visit was due to a complication caused by an infection and he was currently under sedation.

An unexpected sorrow entered Damien's heart on hearing this news, his feelings were still so mixed-up, yet he dared not mention this to his boss. Instead, he grabbed his coat and set off for home. Realising, as he made his way to the car, that the papers they had spent so much time preparing, would have to be reworked if the Don didn't survive. It was with a heavy heart that Damien finally arrived home, having thought about Simona the whole way. Whilst she could not be connected to the crimes, if the Don should die, Simona would inherit his entire estate. However, Damien knew that she would give it all up in a heartbeat, if that meant her father would pull through. Knowing she had been away for a short break in the sunshine to help her de-stress, Damien had been relieved to find out she'd arrived back in the UK a few days ago, so would be home already. In fact, it had been her father who had encouraged her to get away for a short break, having become concerned for her wellbeing following James' untimely death, plus his own recovery and ongoing arrest, awaiting trial.

As Damien's car swept into their drive, Inga was already opening the front door, excitement oozing from every pore as she welcomed her husband home. Ushering him inside, it was obvious to Damien that she had something good to tell him, but before Inga could speak, he kissed her hard, holding his wife in his arms so tightly, as he desperately tried to block out the mental images of the Don and a weeping Simona by his bedside. Thoughts which had invaded Damien's mind all the way home. When Inga finally pulled away from Damien's embrace, she told him she had some wonderful news, but that he must come into the lounge. Why the lounge, Inga didn't really know, but she knew she didn't want to tell him whilst they were stood in the hallway and the lounge was closest. As she led Damien by the hand and pulled him towards the middle of the room, Inga turned to face him. After knowing how ill she had been that morning, Damien was relieved at how much better Inga now looked and in awe of how child-like her mood was. Damien laughed at her and said it was like seeing a kid on Christmas morning, when they realised Santa had been. Feeling slightly out of sorts and very guilty for his earlier thoughts, Damien gave in to his wife's excitement. "Okay, darling, what is it? What is the big news you have to tell me?" Smiling as he stroked her face with his fingertips, Damien thought how very beautiful Inga looked in that moment and his heart swelled with love for her.

"Damien, the most wonderful thing has happened," Inga paused before continuing, carefully watching his face, to gauge his reaction to her next words. "Well, you know I was being so ill this morning without really knowing why?" It felt like a loaded question, but Damien played along. "Well, when Kate came around, we talked about what was causing the sickness, so, we did a test. Well, Kate went out and bought the test and I did it..."

Inga was grinning from ear to ear, "...and, basically my darling, the reason for the sickness is that I'm actually pregnant!" Inga held her breath as she waited for Damien's reaction.

The words, 'I'm pregnant' sank into Damien's mind, pushing out all thoughts of Simona and her father. Instead, his arms circled his wife's waist, pulling her towards him as, grinning, he replied, "Truly? You're really pregnant Inga? You mean we're really going to have a baby?" Damien was relieved, overjoyed and overwhelmed with love for his wife as he hugged her tightly, then released her quickly, apologising, as he stared down at her tummy, before pulling her towards him again, more gently this time and kissing her passionately.

Immense love filled both of their hearts and minds, as they conjoined in a celebration of their new life together, with their very own baby. Inga was filled with love and desire for Damien and with her pregnancy hormones now racing, she wanted to celebrate their news in a more passionate and carnal fashion. As she began unbuttoning his shirt, Damien paused, "We might hurt the baby..."

Inga chuckled, "No, we won't, it's fine. Don't worry my darling, just make love to me, I want you to." Inga was ready for him, her hormones already raging at the anticipation of his hardness penetrating her and she loved him more than ever.

Damien looked into the eyes of his sexy and very horny wife and his own desires erupted, as his mind was flooded by thoughts of this woman, this goddess, who was soon to be the mother of his child.

Inga touched him and his wanton needs turned caveman-like as he pulled the cushions from the sofa, before pushing her down onto them. Lifting her dress up and pulling her panties off, Damien quickly and easily slid into her waiting, warm wetness. Inga groaned with pleasure as the two of them moved into an easy, familiar rhythm, which quickly escalated when Damien fastened the pace, until he felt Inga's orgasm gripping him, whilst his own sperm shot hot and full into Inga's belly. God, he loved this woman so much! As their climax peaked, Damien's face was inches from hers and he whispered the words that Inga needed to hear, "You truly are the most beautiful woman in the world, Inga. I love you so much and you've just made me the happiest man in the world." The two of them were lost in the moment, a precious closeness growing, that no-one could break.

Chapter 11

A Gathering of Friends

As Saturday morning dawned, the weather brightened and it looked like they would be able to use the garden after all. Inga hoped it was going to be a perfect day and so far, it was. Indeed, everything was going really well, until another bout of morning sickness took over. Thankfully though, like the past two days, after a couple of hours Inga felt much better. With everyone expected to arrive around two o'clock, the food plan was to graze throughout the afternoon and evening, with wine and beer in plentiful supply. Inga found that method always worked best for their past gatherings. Everyone loved her food and she loved entertaining, so it was a great mix. Working on autopilot, Inga finalised everything for their gathering of friends. The marinated meat was perfect and a selection of freshly made desserts were already chilling in the refrigerator.

Inga was relieved that Kate and Pete were the first to arrive and after saying their hellos, Pete and Damien headed off to the beer cooler in the garden, whilst Kate pulled Inga into the kitchen to ask how it had gone with Damien and the baby news. Although, as soon as she mentioned the word 'baby', Kate realised she really didn't need to ask anything else, because Inga's eyes filled with happy tears and she smiled the brightest of smiles, whilst nodding at Kate and accepting the hug on offer. Both women were relieved that the baby announcement had been so welcome and were excited that they had such happy news to share with the rest of their friends. They were soon interrupted by the arrival of Shelley and Dave, who had taxied across town with Emily and Jed. As the gathering of friends bonded over drinks in the garden, the smell of delicious food wafted towards them. Inga's cooking meant they were all in for a treat. As the afternoon got going, Inga's joy could be contained no longer and she signalled to Damien, who was ready and waiting to share their happy announcement. Calling everyone to order with the tapping of a knife against his glass, Damien grinned at them while they cheered, "Speech!" With the exception of Kate and Pete, all of them were totally unaware of what he was about to say.

Damien took Inga's hand and gently pulled her towards him. As the two of them turned to face their friends, with one hand held against Inga's tummy, Damien announced, "Friends, we wanted you all to know that, finally" – he paused and grinned – "my beautiful wife and I are going to be parents!" Everyone gasped at the unexpected news and then cheered wildly, as their clapping hands sloshed drinks from their glasses, causing much laughter as, grinning their biggest smiles, they each hugged both Damien and Inga. Following up with jolly comments about how he was a sly old dog and how lucky they were that he wasn't shooting blanks after all.

The laughter and happiness rose to an almost hysterical pitch until Lowry, who had arrived through the back gate and into the garden, mid-cheer, called out, "Hey everyone, what's going on then? Who won the lottery?" As they turned to face her, Damien was hidden from view, but he could see that standing behind Lowry was the very woman he never expected to see again. Yes, there in the flesh, was Simona!

"Oh, my God," Damien's voice was hushed and in all the excitement, nobody heard him as they turned to greet

Lowry and her new friend, Simona. An obviously pregnant Simona!

"Fuck!" The word hissed on his breath so silently that nobody could hear him. As Simona stepped out from behind Lowry, her tummy was all that Damien could focus on.

"Fuck!" The word left his lips again, involuntarily, but thankfully, still not heard by anyone. More importantly somehow, in all the furore, Simona had not yet spotted her James, who was standing in the garden, large as life and very much alive!

Panicking and wondering how he could escape the group, Damien realised he was screwed, totally and utterly. But, more importantly, all of his friends and now his beautiful Inga – *newly pregnant with his baby* – had been dragged unwittingly into his seedy, dirty world of undercover narcotics and gun-running gangsters. Simona must not see him!

As everyone crowded around the new arrivals, they were all chattering excitedly as they shared the happy news and celebrated Inga and Damien's pregnancy.

Somehow Damien managed to sneak past the group and escape into the house, rushing upstairs to the safety of their bedroom. Closing the door behind him, he took out his phone to call Mike Day, who, never off duty, had his work mobile with him. As Damien explained his predicament, the two men decided the safest thing was to get Damien out of the house, but to do that, they had to rope in someone to help keep Simona in the garden and away from any photographs displayed inside. The ruse would be that Damien was being called into work to help with an emergency situation and Pete, it was decided, would be the best person to have as his partner in this sordid arrangement.

Damien text Pete's phone, *'Mate, need you urgently upstairs, don't tell anyone where I am and come alone, just say you're popping into the house to get some more beers or something.'* Damien waited until he could hear Pete's footsteps on the stairs and opening their bedroom door a crack to check it was him, Damien beckoned Pete to come inside quickly.

In about ten minutes flat, Damien had told Pete about his undercover police work, that they'd recently busted a mafia Don and that his daughter was the girl in their garden, the one that Lowry had just brought to the party!

"Bloody hell, Damien! What the heck are you gonna do and how can we get her out of here?" Pete realised the seriousness of their dilemma and was ready to be Damien's back-up. Thankfully, Pete's own military training meant he could understand and accept, without too many questions, the significance of covert operations. Pete was actually the perfect choice to have Damien's back on this one.

Damien outlined a quick plan. "The best thing to do is to let the party ride out and hopefully, she'll leave, none the wiser. But, Pete, for Inga's sake, whatever happens, make sure Simona doesn't wander around the house. I can't afford for her to see any pictures of me. I'll leave now and go straight to Antoine's. My boss will meet me there. If you can just tell Inga that something really urgent came up at work and I've had to rush off, but that I'll be back later. She won't be happy, but that's the best I can think of right now. Call me if anything happens. I can be back in ten minutes flat. The boss is sending an armed squad to watch the house and follow Simona when she leaves and for God's sake, Pete, don't tell anyone about this. All of our lives depend on me not screwing this up any more than I have already!"

With that and his understanding of the seriousness of the situation, Pete told Damien to just go, get out quick and leave it with him. Pete was still oblivious of just how closely involved Damien and Simona had been, but it was the mention of the word 'Mafia' that had grabbed his full attention. Damien nodded and was gone, grateful for Pete's obvious and unquestioning loyalty.

Pete returned to the party in the garden and quietly informed Inga that Damien had been called in due to a high-risk emergency. Pete wasn't lying, to him, this whole thing sounded like one huge fucking mess and Damien sure was spooked by Simona being in his house. Trying to sound calm, he brushed off the seriousness of the situation, feeling certain that Inga would not ask questions in front of everyone; he was right and very, very relieved when she carried on with entertaining their friends. Meanwhile, Pete pretended to be drinking and joining in with the casualness of the afternoon, whilst also watching Simona's every movement. Pete was totally focussed and ready to distract her, should Simona attempt to wander around the house alone. With his mind in overdrive, Pete remembered and was thankful for the downstairs cloakroom being straight off the hallway, which meant it could be accessed via the kitchen. The lounge would have completely blown Damien's cover, with its array of photographs scattered around the room. Pete was careful to loiter unsuspiciously and protect curious eyes from seeing something they shouldn't. Thankfully, Simona, who was a very confident-and-out-there kind of girl, seemed more interested in Lowry, who was now squeezing her arm a little possessively, subconsciously demonstrating how besotted she was with the unquestionably beautiful Simona. The group were surprised and sympathetic to hear that Simona's father was in hospital with an infection, but totally understood that if he needed her today, she may have to drop everything and run. Of course, she had left out the minor detail of just who her father was. Even Simona could do without that kind of attention.

Whilst Pete felt like he had become a spy who was guilty of watching their friends so closely, at the same time, he was enjoying being on full alert and feeling useful again. Also, realising that his military life was something he had obviously been missing alot more than he'd previously thought. Having been medically discharged for what he considered to be an insignificant injury, Pete had retrained for his future, using his military technical and mechanical background, as good grounding to become a helicopter engineer. A career which had served him well by keeping him in a highly-paid, challenging and interesting job.

The armed MI5 squad arrived in a plumber's van, maintaining an incognito presence, so as not to raise any alarm. Luckily, they had been able to park on the opposite side of the road, slightly down-wind from the house. Their orders were to watch and wait, until Simona was seen leaving, then to follow her.

At Antoine's, Mike Day had just arrived and seeing Damien walk in, he ordered black coffees before the two men took the farthest seats away from the bar and listening ears. Thankfully, with Antoine working away in the kitchen, there was no-one to interrupt them as they discussed how best to manage this unexpected issue.

Inside his head, Damien was panicking. This was such an unusual situation for him that he was struggling with it. Mainly because his head and heart were pulling him in different directions, what with the complexities of Simona, Inga, new babies and his now divided loyalty to his work.

As professional behaviours and thinking took over, the two of them managed to hatch a plan of action. The first step being to have the hospital call Simona, saying her father had taken a turn for the worse, following a stroke. That was easy to arrange and Mike got his team onto it immediately.

Twenty minutes later, Simona left Damien and Inga's house, hurrying to her car, which was parked some twenty yards along the road. Following her, as she set off at speed, was the plumber's van, but, with the news that her father had declined, Simona was completely unaware of whoever might be behind her. All she knew was her father needed her and so, without delay, she was on her way to the hospital again, cursing herself for having chosen an afternoon of pleasure with Lowry.

Damien returned to the house soon after Simona had left. Re-joining the party, he apologised to everyone, explaining that his absence was unavoidable – no lie there – and telling Lowry he was sorry to have missed meeting her friend. Pete watched all of this and admired the way Damien so easily slotted back into 'normal' life. Although, still unaware of the turmoil running through Damien's head at what could have happened, had Simona seen him there, Pete was impressed at Damien's professionalism. *Jeez, that was a close call!* The thought ran through both men's heads as they clinked bottles of beer and merged back into the party atmosphere. Lowry meanwhile, was worried and decided to leave the party soon after Simona, wanting to call her new girlfriend to find out how her father was doing.

A dangerous situation was brewing and Damien could only hope that Lowry and Simona did not get any closer. Mike Day had already thought about it though and was, at that very moment, speaking with the Head of MI5 to agree how best they could handle this issue. It was the worst possible situation for them, screwing up an operation that MI6 were also involved in. But, in fairness, this was a situation they had never come across before, having always been most careful to ensure undercover officers lived outside a minimum twenty-mile radius of the area under surveillance. Of course, a random meeting between a customer and flight attendant, which had then led to much more, had not been part of their original risk assessment. The shit had really hit the fan on this one and damage limitation was going to be tough.

The Don's condition had actually deteriorated for real by the time Simona reached the hospital, his infection having really caused him to stroke. Simona rushed to her father's room, only to be kept outside by the armed officers guarding him, she watched in panic as through the glass partition she saw several nurses and doctors crowded around her father's bed, working on him and attaching various different machines and drips to the ailing Don. It became apparent that the effects of his infection had worsened and her father's organs were also beginning to fail. The call went out to Damien's boss, who arrived soon after, before then making his own call to Damien.

"Hi Mike, what's new?" Damien was still with their gathering of friends and tried to make the call sound casual, as he simultaneously signalled that he'd take it inside. Everyone else was, by now, quite tipsy, with the exception of Inga of course, who, knowing she was finally pregnant, was avoiding all alcohol. Pete was still on high alert from his earlier responsibilities and the shock at learning about Damien's real job, so he was also sober, feeling the need to remain so, to watch Damien's back, for today at least. Also, there was no knowing if Lowry and Simona would return unexpectedly. Although in truth, Pete very much doubted that would happen.

Mike Day was back in control of the situation, but for how long, he didn't know, as he advised Damien, "MI6 are totally pissed, we've obviously touched a raw nerve over this bust. It's clear they were counting on this opportunity to take down a major international drugs ring and use it to boost their image with the Joint Intelligence Committee. I'm waiting on guidance as to how we handle this situation and it's coming from the top!"

"Shit! Although, I'm not surprised when you consider how much we pulled in." Damien was referring to the value of drugs and guns they'd prevented from hitting the streets. The Don was obviously not the top of the international tree on this one and as that thought ran through his head, Damien knew he had to be straight with Mike.

"Mike, I've got to tell you more about this. The truth is, I've really screwed up!" Damien winced as he heard Mike's reaction at the other end of the phone.

As he ended their conversation, Mike cursed again and then looked around hurriedly, to check who was within earshot. Mike knew this was about to explode in his face and he wasn't best pleased with that fact, even though he also knew they [MI5], were massively at fault for Damien's dilemma, having instructed him to do whatever it took to gain the Don's confidence.

Simona was crying, she knew her father was about to die and there was nothing more that could be done. Now sat by his bedside, she took his hand and pulled it to her lips, whispering the words, "I love you Papa." As she kissed his hand, the Don sighed and with a final squeeze of her fingers, he was gone from her life, never to return. Simona wailed as the duty registrar confirmed time of death and one by one, a nurse switched off the machines that had been monitoring their now deceased patient. Simona's wails grew louder as the machines fell silent.

Seeing the family of a patient so distraught would normally have touched the registrar's heart, but she knew who this man was and so her sympathy was non-existent. Unsurprising, her clipped response gave away the lack of empathy she felt, as she advised the weeping Simona that whilst they would allow her time to say goodbye, the armed guard would remain at the door.

Damien pulled Pete to one side and asked him to stay sober, but he needn't have worried because Pete hadn't touched a single drop since their earlier discussion – he had even held onto an empty beer bottle, so as not to raise suspicion – wanting to be clear-headed in case Damien needed his help again. Which, as it turned out, he did. Damien told Pete they were both required to attend a debriefing, at least, that is what Damien had been told by Mike. What Mike hadn't said – although Damien knew it would be inevitable, given the circumstances of the day's events – was that Pete would be required to sign the Official Secrets Act, to ensure he did not share any information relating to this assignment. Coincidentally, and unrealised by either Damien or Mike, Pete had already signed and was bound by the Official Secrets Act, following his previous military Special Forces work. Obviously, Damien knew nothing about Pete having been a member of a Special Forces Unit, and neither did Kate. All Kate had ever been told was, that Pete fixed helicopters for the military and several civilian organisations, as well as a few private owners.

When the party came to a natural close, everyone disappeared home, leaving just Pete and Kate behind to help clear up. Although for Pete, the real reason he stayed was to be on-hand for the call from Damien's boss. An hour and a half later, Pete and Damien had cleared the garden and were about to sit back down when the call came in. Inga and Kate were still clearing up in the kitchen. Mike's voice was unusually serious, almost stern, as he confirmed that Damien and Pete were to head back to Thames House immediately.

As Damien's cover for his friends – Kate, in this instance – was that he was a 'Sales Executive', he had to pretend that a major international order had gone belly-up and because it was worth millions, and there was a time difference between the countries involved, he had to go into work straightaway. As Damien explained to Inga once more that he had to desert their marital bed, probably all night, Pete suggested Kate stay over and that he would run Damien into the office, pretending that he was soberer than his host and therefore able to drive. Of course, both of them were sober, but it was a perfect excuse and again cemented the 'normal' life that Damien was trying to portray to Kate. Damien was intrigued at Pete's reactional ability to handle the situation, without fuss and without blowing his cover and decided that would be a conversation for their drive back to 'Thames'.

Chapter 12

Consequences

Now sat in his boss's office, Damien knew the seriousness of this new situation and despite the comfortable, familiar surroundings, he was feeling nervous. Mike's first discussion point was the damage limitation required between Lowry and Simona. They had to work out a way of preventing Lowry from having any further contact with Simona. There was a risk of common photographs being seen and shared, as well as the fact that Lowry would NEVER be able to take Simona anywhere near Damien and Inga. The fallout had expanded though and whilst the end result would be totally unfair on the utterly innocent Lowry, it was very necessary and Lowry's personal happiness could not even be considered.

Damien's heart was sinking ever further into his boots with every realisation of just how complicated this whole sorry affair was. Including the fact that the chance of him being the father of Simona's baby was more than extremely high, it was totally inevitable and that bothered him a lot more than he wanted it to. In spite of the fact that their sex sessions were drug-induced, Damien's memory of them had not faded. In fact, if he was totally honest, he had fantasised about them more than a few times. Mainly when he was alone in the shower, remembering what he had done to the beautiful and very sexy Simona and what she had done to him in her shower. The fact that she was bisexual had never really been a consideration or a concern for Damien because he knew that what he was doing at that moment in time was only ever meant to be temporary. At least, that is what he had convinced himself of, but of course, with his mind having been affected by drugs, using any kind of protection had not even remotely occurred to him. Lust having clearly overtaken any grain of common sense he may have exerted. Now though, all plans of 'temporary' had been trashed and he could only see another baby – his baby – and worrying that he would have to tell Inga. Not that he could ever see the child, he was sure that would be a given, but that aside, his guilt would not allow him to deceive his wife any longer.

As he now had to tell Mike, Damien guessed that Inga, like Mike, would probably never trust him again and the fact that he had been working under orders would be conveniently brushed aside. Damien worried that this admission would not only be the likely end of his career, but the end of his marriage too.

Mike was speaking, his voice growing louder and more demanding as he realised that Damien's mind was drifting, "Are you listening to me? Christ, Damien, this is the biggest fucking cock-up I've ever encountered and YOU are in the sodding middle of it! How the bloody hell we are going to get you out of this one, God only knows and not only that, it's likely I'll be forced to reassign you. Which, by the way, would be even worse for the team, because up until now, you've been my best undercover officer and I was counting on your promotion to train up an elite squad!"

Mike was seething with frustration, anger and disappointment, making his language more raw and coarse than his normal calm approach. Yet, he also knew that Damien's situation had been impossible because the Joint Intelligence Committee had basically authorised that Damien should 'fully improvise' to gain the Don's trust. But, now, with this mess on their doorstep, that convenient authorisation seemed like a lifetime ago and MI5 were left with the explosive collateral damage of Simona being pregnant with, most likely anyway, Damien's baby. Their only saving grace was, that at this moment in time, Simona still thought James was dead and the trauma of his death had encouraged her to run from her grief and reignite her interest in the fairer sex. Namely, Lowry, who, Simona subconsciously considered, was a safer option than another man. Not that Simona was even remotely interested in thinking about another man. No, she was in need of love and nurturing through this tempestuous time in her life and that was a fact no-one could deny. So, it was her liking for the female persuasion, which encouraged her to become involved with the most delicious member of cabin crew that she had ever laid eyes on. Kate's friend, Lowry.

It was possible that Simona would continue her life thinking she had lost James, which would satisfy MI5. Lowry, on the other hand, was a different ball game. How were they going to handle her? That was the burning question which Mike and Damien had to find a resolution to.

Whilst they were deliberating shared ideas, Pete was being held in another room, awaiting senior authorisation to fully disclose his own history and therefore, trustworthiness. There was one blessing at least, knowing that Pete had already signed the Official Secrets Act, left Mike Day feeling utterly relieved. The next step was to try and recruit Pete. MI5 always needed fresh blood and trustworthy new faces were welcomed, particularly when dropped into the lap of MI5. There was a massive operation being planned for the coming months and more agents were needed than they currently had available during that timescale. Someone who had never been used by MI5 before, would be a perfect choice and not only that, gaining an agent with such intensive military training could not have been planned better. But, that was for later. Mike knew he needed to ensure MI6 did not side-swipe Pete and try to steal him for themselves, hence why he was being detained in one of their holding suites, awaiting further discussion and hopefully, buy-in to the job offer they were planning to put to him.

Damien had tried to pump Pete about his working life when they were in the car; realising there was more to Pete than he had previously known, but, like Damien, Pete was also bound by the Official Secrets Act and knew that others' lives depended on his confidence. So, he kept the detail to a minimum, whilst sharing enough with Damien, that without him needing to ask directly, he would realise Pete had previously also had a secret life. Never before had Damien felt so thankful for such a confidence, his instincts told him he could trust Pete and that made him feel a whole lot better. Better, that was, until Simona and her pregnant belly filled Damien's mind again and he fell silent for a while. Meanwhile, as Pete had driven them along the empty night-time streets, his own thoughts had wandered into the unexplained territory of what exactly it was that Damien was involved in. Damien's previous admission obviously not being the full story. It was clear that the two of them needed to talk, but both were silenced and bound by duty.

Mike informed Damien of the plan authorised by the Head of MI5. Neither one of them liked it, but they both knew it to be necessary. Whilst it was obvious that people would be hurt, those same people would not be killed. At least, that was the plan, but which would involve Damien working away from home again, albeit for just a few days this time. Damien assumed Inga would understand, as she always did, but he also knew she was already beginning to make plans for their new future, when he started his new management role. The trouble was, if this didn't end well, Damien knew that his promotion was as likely to happen as Simona's baby *not* being his.

Pete was excited by the offer being handed to him, having realised in the past twelve hours that this adrenaline-filled lifestyle was what he missed, loved and craved. Pete was onboard, without question. Kate crossed his mind, but this was his life, his future and it was real. Pete needed this and he just hoped that Kate would understand and accept his new life. Without her support, Pete realised he was heading for the possibility of a single life, but he hoped that because he wanted to marry Kate, she would want that too and say yes. That way, she and Inga could have each other's back, aware of their joint secret, which might help them both to cope with the periods of absence and worry. Pete signed up there and then, no second thoughts were needed. Now, he just had to convince Kate it was going to be okay. Which was probably going to be easier said than done.

Of course, Kate and Inga would not be able to discuss the details of whatever their men would become embroiled in, because they would only know the absolute minimum required. Which, in reality, was never the truth anyway and was just a cover story to constantly test partners' loyalties and keep them safe from whatever harm their loved one was involved with. But, they could support each other, knowing one or both of their men were fighting for Queen and Country, in the ongoing war against extremely complex crimes and terrorist threats, which were evermore a part of the modern world.

As the recovery mission started, Damien was held back. His role was to listen-in and identify who was who, from the voices heard on the bugs he had strategically placed around the Don's home during his time there.

It had been suggested that Simona might try to step into her father's shoes. Damien hoped not; he knew she had never felt any kind of liking for the seedy side of her father's life, but, it was something they had to check out and if necessary, prevent. Damien knew what that really meant.

Simona was now also grieving for her father, as well as James, so her thoughts were irrational and often bounced wildly between despair, anger and revenge. Something akin to crazy drug-induced balls of emotion. One minute she wanted to run away from the pain and confusion, and the next, she wanted someone to pay for her father's death – it was in those moments that Mike's team listened more intently – understandably, Simona wanted to know exactly who was involved in the drugs raid which had resulted in the fatal bullet wound that finally took her father's life.

Chapter 13

Simona and Lowry

Lowry had just been a flirtation to Simona, a heady experience from an insatiable wantonness, which had seen her entice the short-dark-haired member of crew, into a forbidden sexual encounter in the first class cabin, during a time when other passengers were sleeping. Lowry had been totally smitten by the flirtatious behaviour of her passenger in seat six and had found her utterly irresistible, wanting her from the moment she had helped to stow Simona's over-sized hand luggage in the cabin lockers.

Simona's perfume had been overwhelming, as she had taken Lowry's offered hand, before sitting down gently and very aware that her slightly heaving, enlarged bosom was on full display as Lowry towered over her. Fully aware of the effect she was having on her attendant, Simona's soft manicured fingers had Lowry wanting to kiss them and touch them to her own breasts, allowing them to tweak her nipples until they were hard enough to be sucked into that deliciously, welcoming, warm and smiling mouth. Lowry's head had lost out to her sexual fantasies and she knew, without doubt, that she wanted this woman to feel her own intimate warmth, as her thoughts began an elaborate fantasy, imagining Simona's tongue exploring her most private of places. As she too would then also do to Simona, slipping her own soft, delicate fingers into Simona's wetness and stroking her until the two of them climaxed, silently, knowing other passengers might hear them. The mile-high club would be proven to be alive and well in first class later.

Lowry, of course, had not been able to resist or forget Simona and following their inevitable sexual encounter, she had waited with baited breath until she received that longed-for call from her pregnant, mile-high lover. When Simona's call came, Lowry had been ecstatic. The two women were sexually besotted with each other from their very exciting and totally unexpected encounter, so, to meet up again held an excitement for them both which was full of anticipation at the inevitable prospect of a repeated sexual performance.

After Simona had left the party abruptly, her suggestion that Lowry stay and enjoy the afternoon had been too much for Lowry to follow-through. So, having made her own excuses, she had left soon after to follow Simona, desperate to support her new lover. The hospital had been a long drive – miles away, in fact – but Lowry was undeterred and as she pulled into the car park, she searched for Simona's car, parking as close to it as possible, before entering the hospital to find her.

Simona's father had already passed-over by the time Lowry found them and when she touched the weeping Simona's shoulder and saw the relief wash over her face at the very sight of Lowry, she felt enlightened – convinced that Simona must already love her – as from her seated position, Simona held onto Lowry, crying into her belly, whilst Lowry stroked Simona's long hair, comforting her as best she could and falling for her with every gentle movement. Lowry stayed with Simona until it was time for them to leave and return home.

Mike and Damien had not expected Lowry to show up at the hospital, so they were even more surprised and concerned when they heard Lowry's voice, sounding through the bugs hidden in Simona's house. The two men knew they had to move quickly. Lowry was in the gravest of danger and so were her group of friends, friends that Damien also knew and loved. Once Simona made any kind of connection between James and Damien it would be game over, and the chance of that happening was escalating with every moment which passed. Damien knew he could not intervene, after all, James was dead as far as Simona knew. But, Lowry was going to be his downfall, he just knew it, he didn't need a sixth sense to understand that likelihood. Lowry would end up betraying her friends without even knowing it and most likely, by innocently showing Simona a photograph from one of her social media pages. Mike made the decision to block the Wi-Fi and phone signals to the house whilst they considered how their plan should change. Experienced in thinking on their feet, Mike and Damien were both very aware of how that was so much easier when there was no personal link to the parties involved.

Simona wanted Lowry to stay with her; she needed comforting during this awful time and as Lowry was not back on duty for another week, she was more than happy to oblige. Especially, when Simona pointed out that as they were the same size in clothes, there wouldn't be a problem as far as she could see, because Lowry could just wear some of hers. Lowry was so besotted that she didn't care if her diary clashed at all, she would cancel everything to spend time on cloud nine with Simona. Having showered and changed into some of Simona's clothes, she now sat on the bed, running her hand across it, imagining how later that evening, she would be cuddling with Simona under the bedcovers.

What she didn't know was that, as James, her friend Damien had himself slept and made love to her sexy Simona in that very same bed. Apart from the obvious, the difference being that Simona and James' love making had been hot, steamy, hardcore sex sessions; scenes which would have had Lowry crying with disappointment and disbelief, had she witnessed the two of them performing such erotic heterosexual acts.

Standing up, Lowry smoothed her clothes and went to find Simona, who was in the main kitchen with Eliza and Armand, watching the couple crying and comforting one another, having told them of her father's death.

Explaining that she had brought a friend back to stay over and help her through this difficult time, Simona then left Eliza and Armand to grieve and it struck her how incredibly odd it was, that after all the years she had known them both, she had literally only just realised that they were in fact, a couple. It was unbelievable to Simona that her family's two most loyal employees had never let on to her, but it was obvious in that moment, that they truly loved one another. Simona couldn't believe she had never noticed this fact before, but then, she had not really allowed much time for small talk with them, since growing into a woman herself. Thinking back now, to when Eliza and Armand first came into her father's employ, Simona realised that they had actually been her most stabilising influence and that truthfully, she really did care about them, a great deal. Remembering back to her childhood and how they had so obviously loved and spoiled her throughout her life, Simona felt a little shameful at her selfish behaviour. Of course, Eliza and Armand had hidden their disappointment at her disdainful attitude, as she progressed through her teenage years into the twenty-something beauty she now was. But, having realised she was pregnant and knowing that James must be the likely father, Eliza and Armand now felt truly sorry for her. Simona was alone again, with a baby on the way and now, her beloved father was also gone. Whilst Eliza and Armand did not presume to continue their employment, they hoped and prayed that Simona would keep them on. Which of course, she had not even doubted, let alone thought to allay any concerns or fears that Eliza and Armand might have. The loyal twosome would wait and see how life panned out, whilst they were all grieving.

Leon, Simona's driver, had left the employ of the Don after the shooting, managing to escape the clutches of the gangster family he had been working for, by leaving on good terms during his little holiday. Whilst away from the house, Leon had called and left a message for the Don, explaining that his wife's family, who lived abroad, had asked for and needed his help and which he, Leon, could not refuse. Simona had been doubly-surprised when her father, who understood the pull of family, had wished Leon well and allowed him to resign without further question. The Don had also known he was about to offer James the task of driving him and Simona anyway. So, taking advantage of the situation, the Don paid Leon a leaving bonus for being so loyal and looking after the family so well. Whilst the much-appreciated monetary gift was a drop in the ocean to the extremely wealthy Don, the real gift was that Leon's family could start their new life, without fear of being hunted down and to top it off, enjoy a debt-free future.

As Simona now thought of Leon, happy and with his family, she decided not to pass on the sad news of her father's passing. There was no need for Leon's happiness to be thwarted. That act of kind generosity surprised even Simona, but unbeknown to her, her hormones were in nesting mode and the love she felt for hers and James' child, was stronger than any she had known before. It influenced everything she did. Including, making a promise to herself that life in her home would be different to the Don's and that there would be no more killing, no more trading of drugs, or anything else that was evil. Nothing that was capable of damaging her or her baby would be allowed to happen in that house ever again. Simona's resentment, anger and sorrow at her father's death had subsided briefly, but the need for revenge was still buried deep inside her and that was a desire she would inevitably revisit.

Hearing Simona talking to her staff and their obvious distress at the sad news, Lowry had backed away from the kitchen and walked through to the main living space. The house was amazing, it's modern sprawling design appealed to Lowry, yet it was set deep in the beautiful green of the English countryside. Feeling the warmth of the sun on her skin and the design of the house, reminded Lowry of being in the Mediterranean or Italy. Aside from home, the Med and Italy were her favourite places to visit and whenever she could, Lowry would take herself off there, delighting in the quaintness of the mountain villages, as she explored a little further with every trip.

"Oh, my darling, you look gorgeous in that outfit." Simona had just walked in to find Lowry dressed in white trousers and a vivid lemon silk blouse, which was cut away at the shoulders, showing off her smooth suntanned skin perfectly, as it fastened around her delicate neck. "Beautiful. You look absolutely beautiful." Simona was taken aback by quite how stunning Lowry looked.

Lowry beamed, glad that Simona approved of the choice of clothes, picked from her very own extensive wardrobe. It was fortunate that they were almost the same height and size. Although, having seen so many expensive clothes in such a huge closet and knowing this was Simona's family home, Lowry realised that her new lover was clearly extremely wealthy. A fact which also unsettled her somewhat. Being a flight attendant, even a senior one in first class, Lowry could not match this kind of wealth and that bothered her more than she was prepared to admit.

Simona, unaware of Lowry's concerns and doubts, smiled as she crossed the room towards her. "I shall have to watch out or I'll lose my entire wardrobe!"

Lowry blushed at Simona's little joke. While Simona relaxed as she stepped into Lowry's welcoming embrace and enjoyed the comfort of Lowry's arms, as they firmly encircled the emotional Simona, now tearful again and longing for her father. As Lowry held her tight, Simona sobbed until she had no more tears.

Damien was listening, his heart being torn, whilst realising his feelings and emotions for Simona were still with him. No matter how much he had tried to deny and bury them, hoping if he could do that, they would fade with time, the reality was, on hearing Simona weeping, that Damien still held deeper feelings for Simona than he should. It was undeniable, yet totally understandable on the one hand, because she was a sexual goddess, who had been his very willing and enticing lover, but, on the other hand, he was a married man and had been, when he very first slept with Simona.

Damien realised he was feeling jealous of Simona being in Lowry's arms and shifted uncomfortably in his seat as he listened to their conversation and subsequent love making. Unable to control himself, despite the fact that Simona was with another woman, Damien knew he still wanted her and couldn't deny it. Lowry was in danger though and Damien knew he had to stay focussed on the job. Mentally slapping himself into reality, he forced his growing sexual urges to subside, unsated this time, but knowing that later, he would need to release the pent-up energy he was suppressing right now.

Following the request for a progress report, Damien updated Mike by telephone as to what had been happening, explaining there had been no worrying conversation and that the two women were now sleeping. What he chose not to share was, how the love making session had made him feel and that he now knew, without any doubt, how two women making love was such a turn-on for a heterosexual male! Damien also withheld that he was thankful to have been the only person listening in to that part of their evening and once the two women were sleeping, he had made a beeline for the toilets, desperate to release the built-up sperm that was making his balls ache so much. God, where was Simona's mouth when he needed it so badly. Inga of course, was too perfect, too fragile and not up for that type of release, which meant Damien's lustful thoughts went to the person he knew he wanted most in that moment. *Simona, and after her, Lowry.* Fuck! What was the matter with him? His cock had taken over his mind and being! *No, not your cock, Damien. Simona!* The voice was banging loudly in his head and as his pumping hand felt the sperm shooting out of his rock-hard cock, he'd groaned, a bit too loudly, but luckily, with most of the team already at home in their beds, it hadn't mattered.

Damien had been advised to stay away from Inga until this was over, so, Pete was on call for watching over her, which made Damien feel a little happier. If something happened, he wanted a friendly face to be with Inga in minutes, rather than the couple of hours it would take for him to return home.

Phase one of their plan to remove Lowry would kick-in tomorrow morning and involved getting her out of the house to brief her on just who she was getting involved with. Damien would not be a part of that discussion, which would be managed by Mike himself. It needed someone very senior in MI5 to be able to effectively warn her off, without causing a panic and without Damien's name or identity being revealed. It was crucial that Simona continued to believe that James had died and as long as they could warn Lowry off, Damien, Inga and Lowry, would all be safe.

Chapter 14

An Alternative Story

Mike found that warning Lowry was going to be harder than he had hoped. The two women seemed set for the day and were talking of linking up on social media. Having decided on the storyline, Mike arranged for Lowry to be called back to work on the pretence that an emergency meeting was being called by the airline and Lowry's presence was required. One of the women on Mike's team would make the call. Rehearsed and practised in such matters, it was nothing for an experienced agent to pretend to work for the airline's HR department, explaining that a senior flight crew was being selected to transport various VIPs over an extended period, including the young Royals and their invited guests. The airline meeting and attendees was considered to be highly confidential, so she was not to discuss it with anyone, including her co-workers. The MI5 agent pretending to be one of the airline's HR team explained that this was a really big deal, for all those under selection and so, attendance was mandatory that afternoon for an early briefing and acceptance session.

Timing had been carefully decided so that Lowry realised she would have to go straight to the HR briefing, without even going home first. Perfect. Mike was pleased with his elaborate plan, because it also gave them a good reason for withdrawing Lowry from Simona in the short, medium and long term.

Enjoying a long lie-in with Simona and with nothing to rush their day, after making love for several hours, the two women were having a leisurely brunch on the terrace. As they relaxed in the sunshine, Lowry imagined how she could get used to such luxurious surroundings and Simona's seemingly perfect lifestyle. Admiring Simona, Lowry remarked at how pregnancy clearly suited her. Simona's lustrous hair glistened in the sunshine and her skin positively glowed. Knowing she was bedazzling Lowry, Simona lapped up every compliment showered upon her by her awe-struck lover. The fact could not be ignored, these two women made a gorgeous couple and whilst Lowry felt awful for thinking such a thing, she was thankful that James was no longer on the scene to distract or take Simona away from her.

An unexpected ringing from her mobile phone changed the smile on Lowry's face to one of intrigue and then slight concern, also causing Simona's interest to be piqued.

Lowry answered the call and as Mike had hoped, she was enjoying the feeling of importance that her selection had created and, unable to keep the secret completely, she promptly told Simona that she would have to pop into work for a few hours, because she was being selected for an important job, which was all a bit hush-hush. Mike was actually delighted that Lowry had let this much slip, because it would make phase two of the deception so much easier.

As Lowry drove away from the gatehouse, she was glowing with pride and thinking how all the important stuff in her life just seemed to be falling into place. A new girlfriend, with whom she was already besotted and who seemed to equally adore her too, a lovely new car, which Lowry had recently purchased, and now a new job which sounded super-important, because she, yes, she, had been selected as part of an 'elite crew'. The fall-out from this state of mind was not going to be pretty, once Mike burst her bubble, but, there was nothing they could do to soften that blow.

Mike and his team were waiting down the street in two vehicles, both with blacked-out windows. As Lowry's car drove past, they began to follow her, holding back until she was well away from the house and in a secluded section of the road, before they manoeuvred in front of her car, forcing Lowry to stop. Feeling very afraid at this deliberate act and with serious looking men stepping out of the vehicles, Lowry panicked and froze, her white-knuckled fingers gripping the steering wheel as, within seconds, there were two men on both sides of her car. They opened the driver's door, making Lowry feel even more terrified of what they were going to do to her. This stuff only happened in films, didn't it? Anyone else might have screamed, but Lowry knew that wouldn't do any good, there was nobody around to help and besides, the men were speaking to her politely and calmly, showing her some kind of formal ID card, before asking her to step out of the car. Within seconds, Lowry realised they were obviously not police, although it was clear they were something official, maybe Special Forces or something like that. Ross Kemp's face from *Ultimate Force* flashed before her eyes. *Too much television, Lowry*, she thought, whilst her eyes widened in fear of what might happen next. The voices were firm as they suggested she join them in the back of the van that had been following her and which was now parked behind her car. As the men led her to the rear of the van, Lowry asked what the hell was going on and despite having been shown ID cards, asked again who they were and what they wanted with her. Now feeling very afraid, Lowry knew they would be too strong to fight and besides, one of them had a gun holster under his jacket, that much she did see as they'd approached her car. Inside the van, it was explained that they were in fact working for UK Government Security Forces and without actually saying MI5, Lowry realised that's who they must be. It was explained to her that Simona was being watched, which was why Lowry had come to their attention, because her new 'girlfriend' was actually part of a Mafia family who were under observation. Mike hoped he was giving Lowry just enough information to scare her, so that she would accept and understand their reasons for pulling her out.

Lowry was lost for words, disappointed and shocked to the core, at the explanation and admission that the 'elite flight crew' was just a ruse to get her out unharmed. Furthermore, the explanation they'd used would be the perfect get-out clause, in that she would be able to back off from Simona, by letting her know she was being pulled away for a confidential role, involving the Royal Family. Which also meant, she would be out of circulation for several months, with no contact allowed with friends, or relatives, including Simona.

Christ, this was scary enough stuff, but not only that, in the short period of time between leaving her beautiful Simona and right now, Lowry realised that everything in her exciting and happy world had just been destroyed. As she sat on the seat inside the van, stunned by what she was being told, Lowry looked defiant. Mike wasn't convinced she would believe it, or even go along with it, so she would be watched. But, the story they had given her was that she would have round-the-clock surveillance and protection, to ensure neither Simona, nor any of her mafia connections could make contact. It was enough to scare the living daylights out of Lowry, who, despite her earlier defiance, right at that moment, just wanted to be sick. Mike told her that the recent news-reported drugs bust had resulted in several people being killed and was actually instigated by Simona's father and his cronies.

Again, hoping it would be enough to convince Lowry that she was better off walking away from the whole situation than to risk becoming embroiled in whatever might happen next.

Although Lowry was still in a state of shock, being a sensible kind of person and one used to high levels of responsibility, she actually understood the seriousness of what she was being told and that it was not something she would be able to discuss with anyone else. Whilst her sensible head took in what Mike was telling her, Lowry's heart was breaking and like a glass, shattering in slow motion to a thousand pieces. Lowry needed to be sick and as they let her out of the van, she rushed to the side of the road and emptied her stomach. Mike watched, feeling a glimmer of remorse at the pain he knew he had just caused, but also knowing it was very necessary. Handing her a clean hanky, he suggested she make her way home, having established that Simona did not know where she lived, or even her last name. Those two facts came as a huge relief to Mike, knowing it would be all the more difficult for Simona to find Lowry, once they'd cut off her mobile and reassigned a new number to her. Thankfully, without her last name either, all the usual social media channels would draw a blank on any searches Simona might carry out. The only sticking point was the airline, if Simona considered trying, she could actually find out that Lowry had not been reassigned and that she was actually still hosting first class on long-haul flights. That was a risk Mike was prepared to take, having decided that if Lowry could sell the storyline to her, Simona would have no reason to call up the airline.

Damien knew all of this was going to happen, but he also knew that he could not speak to Lowry about it. If she had any inkling that he was James, his life would be in danger once again, along with the lives of all their friends.

Damien felt sorry for Lowry though, he knew how heartbroken she would be because he was already feeling that way himself. Simona had a powerful pull, which they had both been beguiled by.

Damien wondered how Lowry would cope with the destruction of her newly-found love and the realisation that the promised, exciting and special job was all a ruse. But he need not have worried so much. Having had to deal with multiple let downs and disappointments in her life, Lowry, was able to accept and understand the situation. Although, it did not help her heart when she later realised just how much she had fallen for Simona. Their encounter had almost certainly been a case of love at first sight for Lowry and that was something she would need time to recover from.

As Lowry watched the vehicles drive away from her, she also wondered when her 'babysitters' would appear. The answer to that question came the moment she arrived home. A pale blue saloon car was parked across the road and as she pulled up, Lowry could see one female agent sat at the wheel, pretending to apply her make-up, with a male sat in the back seat.

Back inside her home, Lowry knew she would never be able to see Simona again and finally, releasing her pent-up emotions, she flung herself on her bed and cried. A couple of hours later, having cried out all of her tears and knowing she had to weave the storyline of being called away to Simona, Lowry could also not bear to have that conversation and so she waited until she knew Simona would be sleeping and with her mobile switched off. Later that evening, Lowry called and left a voicemail, explaining about the new confidential role and telling Simona that she was sorry, but it was too good an opportunity to turn down and whilst they'd had fun, Lowry had to accept the job offer. Thanking Simona for their wonderful time together, she explained that she would return the borrowed clothes by post. As Lowry cried herself to sleep that night, her heart was breaking, for the life she thought she could have had with her perfect Simona and the fact that her actual life was now trashed.

Damien and Mike breathed a sigh of relief as their plan and Lowry's storyline seemed to be working. But, it was early days and the pull of lust and love might prove too much, so they had to keep a close watch on both women. The next few weeks would be critical.

When Simona picked up Lowry's heart-breaking call, she slumped onto her bed and sobbed, feeling utterly dejected and miserable, self-pity took over and she wailed, "Why does everyone leave me?"

As the days ticked by, Lowry's life returned to normal-before-Simona. Whilst for Simona, life was distracted by funeral arrangements and the sorting out of her father's estate. It was a long job, but one which was clearly detailed in the will that their family lawyer held. A blessing which Simona was very grateful for because she really didn't think she could take much more stress, or loss.

The day of the funeral arrived and undercover agents moved into place along the planned route that the cortege would take. The cemetery was also full of disguised agents, some posing as grieving relatives of the long-since buried, others as gravediggers, working on a nearby plot. It seemed ironic that 'life' was busy in that cemetery.

The cemetery was huge and very old, historical in many ways, with several famous residents said to be buried there. It was the place Simona's father had dictated that his remains should be laid to rest, beside his beloved wife, Maria.

Simona knew her father was one for tradition and she did him proud, arranging everything exactly as he had wanted, even down to the beautiful display of white roses, freesias and lilies which adorned his elaborate coffin and the horse-drawn glass carriage that carried him to his final resting place. Identical flowers had also been placed on his darling Maria's grave. Simona was beside herself. Feeling weak from the emotion of the day. Losing and now saying goodbye to her father, she was also still grieving for her darling James, whose funeral she had not been invited to.

The people attending her father's funeral were mainly from the underworld and therefore used to the presence of police. In fact, they expected it. Simona however, was angry about it and spat at Mike as she walked past him. Mike had made sure he was visible at the back of the ceremony; he wanted the accumulated guests to know he was nobody's fool, he knew who they were and they knew it. But, for that day, he could not touch any of them and they relished that thought.

Needing to identify voices of known associates of the Don, Damien was also listening in, along with the regular members of their surveillance team. Using a suitably disguised van, they were parked a short distance along the street, away from the cemetery gates. Although designed to look like an innocent enough vehicle, the van was full of high-tech listening equipment and monitors, which displayed the visuals from the discreet body-cameras that Mike and his team were wearing. Tensions were high and everyone was on full alert, watching and waiting for the slightest wrongdoing and listening for any words spoken out of place. They needed this day to go smoothly, taking every and any opportunity to photograph and note everyone who was there, so the van surveillance team could cross-check identities before mourners left the crematorium. Other gangster families were present and everyone was watching everyone. It was like nothing you would expect in England, but times had changed; gangsters and mafia were one and the same, it was a disease that was spreading throughout London and the Home Counties. That was an absolute fact.

Mike was anxious that nothing should kick off between the families, but there were likely to be people there who were wanted for questioning and they were the ones Mike and his team wanted to pick up. The trouble was, arresting people at funerals was never a good thing to happen and never received well. Personally, Mike couldn't give a toss about the dignity he would normally afford bereaved relatives because this Don had ruined many a young life and murdered many more in his drug-trafficking past, and that was without the many deaths caused by the guns he had also trafficked. Mike wanted whoever he could get from this gathering, but he didn't want all-out war between the families gathered. It frustrated the hell out of him that they had to hold back, but he had to ensure his team played it by the book; they could afford no messing up this time. Everyone involved had been well briefed and knew the score. They would not let him down, of that Mike was certain.

However, life was never simple and rarely went completely to plan when criminals were involved. So, it should not have surprised Mike when one of the families sent men to investigate all parked vehicles within the same street. As they came upon the van that Damien and three others were in, the MI5 agents fell silent, listening to the voices talking outside. Seconds later, their van began to violently shake; two of them fell off the stools they were perched on and yelped as equipment fell and hit them on the head and legs. Damien knew they couldn't get into the van, but he also knew their cover was blown. If they tried anything, he'd have to forego his cover and risk being recognised. Damn, he should have thought of wearing a disguise, at least he could have blended into an unrecognisable array of arms and legs as an inevitable fight broke out. Sure enough, the gangsters lit an oily rag and stuffed it into a ventilation point. The burning oil made their eyes sting and the three men had no choice but to stumble out onto the road. The ensuing fight they had expected kicked off and before they knew it there were six of them involved, all at each other's throats. Radio silence was broken as other agents were instructed to help them.

The service was coming to an end and the mourners were due to move to the cars. Mike knew before it even happened, that Simona was bound to glimpse her James in the fight and sure enough, as her car drove closer to the fighting group, she caught sight of him. Shocked, Simona screamed out, "Stop the car!"

Damien knew she'd seen him, he'd heard her scream, so he immediately slipped into character, limping over to her car as he simultaneously beamed at her. Simona almost sprang out from the car into his arms and as he held her tightly, Damien whispered, "Simona, I can't believe it's you, I tried to get to the cemetery, but they've been following me everywhere, I didn't know what to do, where to go. Oh, Simona!" Playing his part well, Damien buried his head into her hair, delighting in the smell of her perfume, wondering if he could fool her with an on the fly explanation of his absence and now presence, at her father's funeral. They quickly climbed into her car and drove away from the fracas. Slipping back into character came easy to Damien, as he began explaining that with all the dead being ferried to the hospital in body bags following the shooting, there had been a lot of confusion and he had accidentally been wheeled into the viewing area reserved for the deceased patients. It was a couple of hours before he was found to still be alive, by which time he'd suffered significant blood loss and was transferred to intensive care, where he'd remained until they could remove the bullet. On recovery following the surgery, Damien explained that he'd suffered temporary memory loss, not uncommon apparently, but which returned suddenly when, on reading the papers, he saw a photo of Simona and her father. Funeral details were included in the article, which is how he came to be there. Trying to cement his story into Simona's belief, Damien reiterated how seeing her had triggered his memory and he'd desperately wanted to join her at the funeral. The remainder of the web of lies he'd weaved was that on rushing towards the cemetery gates, he suddenly found himself involved in an altercation between police and gangster members. One which was also still taking place as they were driving away from the scene.

Hoping that Simona would believe his lame storyline, Damien was actually shocked when she seemed to. After all, it was so extreme that he didn't believe she would, but Simona never even doubted James would make it up. Besides, she was so happy to have him back that all she could say was, "James, I just can't believe you're alive, I thought you were dead, I thought I'd lost you…" Before she could finish, Damien kissed her hard and seeing tears of happiness squeezing out from under her lashes, his heart melted. Wrapping his arms around her, Damien held Simona tight as she cried emotional tears of sadness, yet relief and happiness, into his shoulder. The driver of their limousine was discreet and pretended not to watch or listen to what was being said, and done, in the back of his car. Being an agent himself, he couldn't believe the story James was spinning and admired his gall. No way could he have pulled off that explanation and have Simona believe it, no way. But, what the driver was not aware of was just how strong Simona's feelings were for James and that her judgement was impaired by that love for him and her pregnancy hormones.

Mike had been informed of Damien's actions and worried for his safety. Ever thankful for Damien's vast undercover experience, Mike just hoped his best officer could pull off whatever explanation he was feeding Simona. The priority now, was for Mike to get back to Thames and listen in to the conversations at the house.

Damien helped Simona from the car and thanked the driver, who winked and wished him luck. Remembering the listening devices that he had planted, Damien knew he had to be careful of what he said. Despite knowing the baby was no longer a secret back at Thames, he was protective of the fact that the majority of the team still did not know it was definitely his baby.

Simona was blooming, which meant it was obvious where their conversation was going to go. Damien knew he had to stay in character, so, he pretended how some things were still foggy to him, explaining that the doctors had told him his memory was likely to return slowly and that different things could trigger his memories and recollections. Blinded by a mixture of relief and love, Simona didn't question James because she totally believed him. There was no doubt for her and knowing that James was trying to get to her father's funeral to support her, made Simona love him even more. James' kiss had already told her that he loved her and Simona absolutely believed that he truly cared for her father too.

Eliza and Armand were as shocked as Simona when they too returned home to find James alive and well. Having travelled in a separate car to their mistress, who had insisted on travelling alone after reassuring them that it was only because her grief was too raw to share with anyone, even them. Eliza and Armand hugged James and welcomed him home. They too were enthralled by the explanation of his absence. Of course, the gun battle had been played down to them, but they had known that James must have been guilty of whatever crime their boss had been involved in. Curiosity overwhelmed them as they now questioned his part, only to be swiftly side-tracked by a request from Simona to leave them, so she could be alone with James. Of course, this request was granted without further question and the two returned to the kitchens to privately discuss their reasoning for James' absence.

As they were left alone once again, Damien took Simona's hands in his, he was clearly overjoyed at seeing her pregnant belly. Simona was glowing. Damien smiled at her and holding her fingers to his mouth, kissed both hands, telling her how happy he was to see her again.

A big fat tear escaped from Simona's eyes as she laughed and said, "Don't worry, these are tears of joy, my darling James."

Damien smiled back at her and kissed her tears away; he could not believe what was happening and had no idea how he was going to escape this time, or even if he wanted to. Time, he needed time, to think.

Kissing Simona again was his natural instinct and as she responded so warmly, Damien found himself picking her up in his arms. Even with the baby inside her, she was as light as a feather to him. Carrying her towards a different bedroom, Damien told her how happy he was and how he could not believe his memory had kept him from her and that he needed to hold her in his arms all night. Despite the oncoming evening, it was still early for bed, but Simona did not care, she wanted to hold James to her own naked skin and to feel his naked skin, she had missed him so much.

Lowry was now far from her mind, cast away, a forgotten memory.

Damien had been cautious about the ears that would be listening in and knowing that Simona's room was now bugged, he chose one which was not as he laid her on the ample bed. Watching her face as he undressed, Damien knew he had to persuade her of his loyalty, but he need not have worried, for there could be no doubt of that. Simona had gasped as she saw him growing with pleasure and passion. Bending forward, Damien ran his fingers from her ankle to her thigh, pushing up her buttoned dress to feel the lacy panties she loved to wear. As his thumb massaged the lace, Simona groaned and began undoing her dress, exposing her beautiful soft tanned skin and full belly, boasting their baby, his baby. Simona wanted him and although Damien was afraid of hurting her, she assured him the doctors had told her that making love was fine, so long as she wanted to, and she did, want to, with him, right now. Damien's reactions were begging for her wetness as he pulled off her panties, then slipping two fingers inside her, he massaged her and gently opened her up, ready to take him. Simona held out her hands and as he took them, she pulled herself up, moving to a kneeling position in front of him, he knew she liked this position and as he gently entered her, Damien's hands reached around Simona's body, searching for the hard nipples he had admired on her swollen breasts.

Simona wanted him desperately, "Harder James, harder, you won't hurt me, it's fine," As Damien's confidence grew, so did his cock and before long he was pushing into her, enjoying her gasps as his thrusts continued harder and faster, before finally exploding and filling her with hot sperm. Simona climaxed at the exact same moment and buried her face in the bedcovers to hide her scream of ecstasy. God, she had missed this, missed James and his fantastic cock; she was also slightly amazed that they had done this without the drugs she normally fed him. Damien had forgotten Inga, he had forgotten Mike, in fact, his aching balls had proved to him that he was infatuated with Simona. Damien lusted after her in his fantasies and even now, as he was pulling out of her wetness, he loved her. Yes, he loved her and he wanted to share their baby!

Damien was done for, his alter ego had taken over his real-life and he knew he was in big trouble.

Chapter 15

Sacrifices

Damien woke up early, having stayed all night with Simona. Now relishing the fact that he was beside her, Damien moved to curl up against the soft skin of her back and gently pulled her towards him, so that her skin was against his muscular chest and abdomen. As his own legs curled in an almost foetal position, Damien knew his role as James had completely taken over his senses. But, even as his arms encircled the sleeping Simona, he knew, without any doubt, that he could never give her up. With his ever-present lust, he wanted her and needed her, on a daily basis and he was not prepared to walk away from her, or his baby. Damien ached to feel their baby move as his hand rested on Simona's swollen belly, hoping and waiting for a little kick.

Simona stirred, her senses awakening, aware of James lying behind her, holding her and stroking her baby belly. "Mmmm... good morning my darling." Simona covered Damien's hand with hers as she pressed herself against the hardness that was making its presence felt between her legs.

Damien murmured into her hair, "Oh, my darling Simona, you are so beautiful and all I ever want. I need you my darling, both of you. I can't let you go again." And, so it was, right there, in that very moment, the place in time when Damien permanently crossed the line, leaving behind his thoughts and love of Inga, who was not even on his radar in that moment, as lust overtook his senses completely and he again penetrated Simona's warmth, holding her gently, as he pushed up into her, again and again. Simona was oblivious to everything, except the man she was in love with and now enjoying morning sex with; her normal sexual appetite was insatiable, but with her pregnancy hormones, there was no stopping her want and need of this, of James and no-one was going to take him from her again, ever. As the two of them reached orgasm together, Simona knew she was the happiest she had ever been in her life, she felt sexy and loved and had her James back again.

Mike Day had just arrived in the office, already feeling very worried. Damien had always been his best undercover agent and was a man he considered a friend, but this job had been different and Mike knew Damien was in too deep, that much was obvious and very disturbing to Mike. The guys listening in overnight had heard nothing, which triggered alarm bells in Mike's head; Damien was so obviously sleeping with Simona and knowing which rooms were bugged, he would have used a 'safe' bedroom. Which confirmed Mike's worst fears, as he resigned himself to the fact that Damien and Simona had been, and probably were still, lovers. As Mike mused on what he could do about it, he realised the options were limited, extremely limited and he knew they would likely involve him losing Damien. This was not good. Mike was pacing as he thought through the best options, still blissfully unaware that Damien had already declared his love for Simona and was, at that very moment, consummating his promise of love for her, sealing his own fate, as well as Simona's.

"What a fucking mess!" Now venting in his empty office, Mike was angry and frustrated at how this had all come about. Throwing his car keys across the desk and simultaneously slinging his coat on the chair beside it, he sat down hard. Mike reached for the handset of the desk phone perched in front of him, then changed his mind and used his mobile phone. There was no going back, damage limitation was wrecked; he now just needed Damien out of there and fast.

Damien's mobile rang. *Shit, I forgot to turn the bloody thing off.* Damien panicked as Simona begged him to ignore it, but he couldn't, the chosen ringtone meant it was Mike and Damien's conscience wouldn't allow him to ignore Mike's call. Scrabbling for his trousers, Damien pulled them on and took the phone outside of the bedroom. There was no way he could risk Simona hearing their conversation.

The discussion was coded, but Damien knew Mike was both worried and angry; he had heard that tone in Mike's voice before and knew it meant bad news. Damien knew Mike had every right to be angry with him, but hoped that somehow, Mike could find a solution to resolve the fallout. Agreeing to come in immediately, Damien confirmed that Mike would see him shortly. Now needing to excuse himself, without raising any suspicions from Simona, Damien found an explanation and quickly dressed, promising he wouldn't be long as he kissed Simona goodbye.

Still on cloud nine, Simona accepted Damien's reason for having to shoot out, not doubting his mood or motives, as she almost glided across the bedroom, wrapping a robe around herself before making her way back to her own room to shower and change.

Feeling the delightful warmth of reassurance and confidence fill her heart and mind, Simona was comforted by the fact that James had declared his love for her. No longer seeing a future alone, James' love and their baby was all that mattered to her right now. Simona smiled, life was moving forwards in a direction she could have only dreamed of a few days ago, when Lowry left. Oh, yes,

Lowry, she mused at how convenient it was that her new lover had been called away. Simona was almost relieved and although she knew she would miss the deliciousness of Lowry's body, it mattered not, because now, she had her James back and all was well again.

Driving into London at speed, Damien thought about the previous night and that morning and how passionately he and Simona had consummated their love. Inga was his wife and he did love her, but Simona, well, she was something else and he just could not give her up. Damien thought about Inga and how different the two women were. *Was it possible to love two women at once?* Whilst he knew he loved Inga and cared about her very much, this whirlwind had turned his life upside down and he was totally and utterly in love with Simona. Yes, that was the difference, he was in love with Simona, whereas his love for Inga could no longer be described in that way. Of course, being a man *in* love, Damien did not appreciate that years of loving someone could change a man's view of that woman and the very description of the way they loved them. It did not compare to the exciting first stages of lust-in-love, which was like a drug addiction and often screwed around with a man's head. Damien thought how he could walk away from Inga and spend his life with Simona; imagining that whilst Inga would be hurt, he would dismiss any sense of guilt by thinking of it as being a natural end to their recent marital problems. That and all being fair in love and war. Inga was a grown up after all. But, because Damien was now thinking with his little head and not the big one on his shoulders, he had somehow forgotten the very important fact, that Inga was also pregnant with his baby.

Mike was suitably anxious when Damien finally showed up and the two of them went into his soundproofed meeting room; nobody outside could hear what was being said, but Damien's colleagues had watched as he walked straight into Mike's office. All of their eyebrows raised as they glanced at each other, each of them wondering what was going on, having seen the worried looks on both men's faces. Those were faces they all knew well and were usually pretty good at reading, but with no inkling of what Damien had done, they were left in limbo, waiting for the briefing session that would no doubt follow.

Taking their seats at the long meeting-table, Mike started; he was rarely slow in coming forward when he had something he wanted to say, "Okay, tell me the truth Damien, and I mean the whole truth, I don't have time for any bullshit!" Mike was in no mood for wool being pulled over his eyes. There was no need for him to worry though because Damien was ready to spill the beans and tell him everything.

As the conversation expanded, Mike totally blew his stack; he was furious at both himself and Damien. It had been him, Mike, with his orders from above, that had put Damien into this impossible position in the first place, but whilst they'd instructed him to do whatever it took to get close to the Don, what they didn't expect was for Damien to have gone and fallen in love with Simona. But, not only that, he had also impregnated her and was now talking of leaving Inga! Who, by the way, was also pregnant with the very baby they had always longed for. Could this shitty mess get any more complicated? Mike could see his own head rolling because of this one. There was no way the powers that be would tolerate this level of catastrophe. They were both in deep shit and whilst there was no way he wanted either of them to lose their jobs, Mike knew that at least one of them would have to go, probably both.

Being in the throes of new love, Damien was not as sad as he expected he would be. Yes, there was some regret because he had always loved his job, but, a future with Simona would be so different to the one he had lived up until now. With the money Simona had, they could go anywhere, do anything – she had already said as much, suggesting they move away and make a fresh start in a different country, somewhere warmer – it was a perfect solution and Damien was totally sold on their plan.

On the journey back to Thames, Damien thought hard about what he was about to do. Whilst recognising that he was totally compromised by continuing to see Simona, he also knew he could never give her up. Which meant there was no way Damien could stay in his MI5 role. Following his declaration of love for Simona and Mike's response, Damien thanked Mike for the support he had always given him during his time at MI5 and offered his immediate resignation. Mike was totally gutted, although, not surprised. They both knew that it really was the only way forward for them now. There was no way Mike could save Damien's job, so with a heavy heart, Mike accepted his resignation, taking Damien's gun and ID from him. Grateful that Damien was very aware of the process, Mike officially stated that Damien must exit the building immediately and that he would be watched on every monitor, until he stepped out of Thames House and into the sunshine.

The two men shook hands one last time and as Mike voiced his personal regrets, Damien matched them. Leaving the room, Damien was only able to nod to his colleagues on his way out of the main office. Protocols were that the person leaving was not allowed to speak to anyone on the way out and that any desk contents would be cleared later, with personal effects being sent on to the person leaving. From his office, Mike watched the monitors showing the corridors and entrance to the building, immense regret showering over him as he saw Damien step outside; his best agent and former good friend, now gone. Mike was gutted. *Damn Simona and damn her father, if he had not been the criminal he was, none of this would have been needed, nor ended up with Damien having to leave.*

Pete had also seen Damien leave and like the others, was completely unaware of what was going on, but he felt certain they would catch up soon enough as he continued with his work.

The air outside had a coldness to it that made Damien pull his jacket closed, before hurrying off to his car, which was parked a few streets away. Having been fully aware of the only course of action Mike could take, Damien had not even parked in the secure underground garage. Now, having already chosen a life with Simona, Damien knew the next stop for him was to tell Inga. That was a conversation he knew would be even harder than the one he'd just had with Mike, but Damien did at least have the good grace to accept that he owed Inga a face-to-face admission, before he packed a few essentials and walked out of their home for good.

With lust and love overruling his normally sensible head and the thrill of Simona waiting for him, Damien was thinking through how the discussion would go and decided that all he needed to bring away with him was a few clothes, he would leave Inga everything, she would need it and she deserved it. Guilt would kick in the moment he saw her, Damien knew that too, but he was fuelled-on by the desire for his new life with Simona and so he continued with his plan. With his foot pressing down on the accelerator as he left London again, Damien called Simona to tell her he would be a little while longer because he was going to collect his things and then return to her. Simona was overjoyed and told him to take all the time he needed; she didn't care about him being late because she was ecstatic that James was coming to live with her. Not knowing of his real life, or that he was already married, Simona had assumed that James was just giving up a rented flat. Well, rented, or owned, it mattered not to Simona, who, thanks to her father's secret investments, was already worth millions.

Inga was in the spare bedroom, preparing the room for the arrival of their baby. Despairing at the fact that Damien had not been home for so long, but, comforted by the knowledge that this was his last job and that very soon, he would have the long-promised desk job, making their future secure. Inga was proud of her husband and she knew that Damien was working hard to provide for her and their new baby. The baby she had longed for and finally, by a miracle, was now growing inside her ever-expanding belly. As she pulled the old trunk from the closet, Inga winced, a sharp twinge momentarily took her breath away, then passed, leaving her thinking she ought to be more careful. Dismissing it and thinking she was fine, Inga opened the trunk, smiling at every tiny item as she began unloading all the precious little outfits she had been collecting, ever since finding out she was expecting their first baby. Marvelling at the cuteness of every little thing as she held each one up, Inga made a mental note of what she had and still needed to get. As those happy thoughts passed through her mind and transformed into the warm glow she felt inside, Inga mused, knowing that she could actually get pregnant now, there was nothing to say they couldn't have a second baby after this little angel arrived.

Rubbing her belly, Inga spoke to her unborn child. "You know, little one, you have a Mummy and Daddy that love you very much and we just cannot wait to meet you."

Another twinge, this time Inga gasped as the pain intensified, it was not at all expected – the baby was too early for labour – Inga grimaced then cried out as she clutched the bedcovers until a third pain passed. Now worried that she had strained herself pulling the trunk out, Inga sat on the edge of the bed, but the pains returned with a vengeance and she cried out again, this time, slipping to the floor as she writhed in agony, petrified for her unborn child, knowing it was too early.

"Nooooo…" Her cry was blood-curdling.

Through the open window, a young woman passing by heard the noise and stopped, then, hearing Inga cry out again and now very concerned, she called out, "Hello! Are you okay? Hello! Do you need help?" There was no response, so the woman rushed to the front door, banging hard as she yelled out again. Inga was being gripped by pains so strong, she couldn't speak and then she fainted. Now unable to hear or respond to the young woman banging on the door downstairs. With no response, but clearly extremely worried by the scream she had heard, the woman did not give up and banged on the door again, before hurriedly searching in her bag for her mobile phone. At that very same moment, Damien's car swept into the driveway and feeling a huge sense of relief, the young woman waved anxiously at the driver, urging him to hurry.

Disturbed by the scene in front of him, Damien leapt from the car as the woman rushed towards him. Explaining what little she knew in a panicked voice, she was relieved again when she saw that Damien had keys and offered to wait whilst he went in to check on the screams she had heard. Reassuring the woman, Damien thanked her for her concern and said not to worry, that he would take it from here. The last thing he needed was a strange woman hanging around today, this day was going to be hard enough. But, reluctant to leave until she knew all was well, the woman waited anyway, now needing to know what had happened and if the woman she had heard screaming, was okay.

Hearing a shocked, "Inga!" coming from the upstairs window, the young woman realised her help might be needed after all and called out to Damien, asking if she should call an ambulance, to which he shouted, "Yes!"

Cradling Inga in his arms, Damien watched as the blood running from between her legs seeped along the carpet. Desperate for Inga's life and that of their baby, Damien's prior resolve melted and tears filled his eyes as his beautiful wife lay unconscious in his arms.

The woman shouted up that the ambulance was on its way. Damien was overwhelmed with worry and despair, unable to respond. *What a fool he had been. No, correction, a brainless fucking idiot whose head and heart had been shot to pieces by his own selfish, sexual needs. Now, two innocent women were caught up in his mess and Inga, his poor beloved Inga, was bleeding badly.*

Damien's own heart was pumping adrenaline as he held Inga in his arms, not knowing what to do for her, whilst the young woman who was still outside, waited, hesitantly, wondering what she should do, then deciding she should wait by the roadside to flag down the ambulance. Feeling thankful that she was there to help, whilst the young woman appreciated she didn't know these people at all, she also knew they needed help right now and so, she was glad to be there for them.

The ambulance arrived within ten minutes and two paramedics jumped out, entering the house through the front door, which had luckily not clicked shut, they called out before taking the stairs two at a time, rushing to the room from where they could hear Damien calling, "In here! Please hurry!"

All Damien could confirm was that Inga was his wife and he'd found her unconscious on the floor, she hadn't opened her eyes and the blood loss was obviously too much – even Damien could see that – he knew they were losing the baby that she had so desperately wanted. Damien's own heart began breaking; for his stupidity, his beautiful and loyal wife *and* their unborn baby. Tears turned to sobs which racked his body as he cradled Inga.

The paramedics took over, attaching a drip as they did all their usual checks before then loading Inga into the ambulance. Damien climbed in beside her, holding her hand as they made their way to hospital. What would they do now? Damien knew Inga would never forgive herself for losing their baby and he worried if she could possibly ever recover from the shock of it – if she even lived – and as that thought passed through his mind, Damien's tears fell again, for their unborn baby, for his beautiful Inga and because of the incredible mess he had created in their lives.

Yet, even in this moment of darkest despair, Simona's face shone through and Damien knew he still had to leave Inga. The only question now was when? When would ever be the right time to leave his beloved wife if she lost their baby?

Damien knew he deserved every bit of this pain and crucified himself for having behaved so badly, as he also wondered how Inga had stayed with him for so long, through all the years of his work taking priority over their marriage. *Man, how much more fucking selfish can you get!* Damien checked himself, what the hell was happening to him? This wasn't who he was, or who he wanted to be, a man worried for his own future, when his unborn baby had most probably just been lost and his wife very likely to go crazy with grief once she woke up.

157

"Oh my God, she will wake up, won't she?" In his panicked thinking, Damien pleaded with the paramedic to reassure him, but it was too soon to tell and so, like them, Damien would have to wait and see what happened once they reached the hospital.

With blue lights flashing and the siren going the whole time, it was a good fifteen minutes before they reached the emergency department. Having called ahead to warn the medical teams of their imminent arrival, the paramedics quickly unloaded the trolley and whisked Inga into resus. Damien had run alongside and as they handed over their patient and the medics took over, he was left watching from the other side of the doors, alone, yet desperate for Inga to survive. Damien had realised their baby was already lost. The nurse who showed him to the relative's room was kind, but Damien barely acknowledged her as he sat on one of the soft chairs hugging the walls of the room. Damien was in shock at how the day's events had unfolded and now, he didn't even know whether Inga was going to survive, or not. It was too much. Damien hated himself for what he had done. This was his fault. The sense of guilt and blame overwhelmed him, a seemingly subconscious attempt at some kind of recompense.

Inga's blood loss had been extensive and extra bags were being ordered. It didn't help that hers was AB negative, the rarest of blood types, so supplies were not as readily available as the medical team would like. It would be several hours before they knew if the emergency surgery had been successful, or even if Inga would fully recover. Damien was warned that she would be very weak and even if she did survive, the road to recovery would be long and painful, particularly when she found out that the baby she had lost was in fact, twin girls.

Reeling from the shock of what he was being told and knowing he could not just walk out now and go back to Simona, Damien's heart was torn into pieces, as his mind took in the knowledge that they had lost two baby girls. Finally, he too, broke down and as the months of stress and torment racked his body, Damien cried like a small boy desperate to be cuddled by his mother, hoping she would reassure him that everything would be okay and that it would all work out fine. But, it wouldn't, and Damien's mother wasn't there to comfort him. If anything, had she still been alive, she would have been ashamed of his recent behaviour. A fact which now made his guilt all the more difficult to swallow. It was a good hour later, before Damien could pull himself together enough to call Simona, although he had no idea of what possible excuse he could give this time. How could he tell her that his pregnant wife had just lost their baby daughters – babies that he had so easily been able to dismiss from his memory whilst he had been lying beside Simona – and their mother, his wife, was now undergoing further surgery to repair a ruptured uterus?

Damien knew he really was on his own now. With no Mike to call for back-up and the lack of his comfortable, familiar, reassurance and understanding of Damien's predicament, made it feel all the more painful by its absence. Damien knew he had to work this one out for himself. The trouble was, it meant more lies and he really didn't want to do that anymore, he was sick of all the lies. The life he had led as an undercover agent was behind him, or at least, Damien wanted it to be. But, more lies meant more deception and now, on this day, it had all blown up in his face. Not knowing what to do for the best, Damien prayed for forgiveness, for understanding and for guidance. Not that he felt he deserved any one of those things, but most of all, he wanted Inga's forgiveness and understanding. Damien needed some kind of spiritual intervention to provide guidance and help him sort out the mess he'd caused.

The fact that Mike had managed to call off the wolves, despite knowing that Damien was going to feature in Simona's life, was help enough. Although, Damien felt he had earned that amount of support following his years of loyal service, living in constant danger and for following the orders which had triggered this situation, but, this request, this desperate plea for help, was too much to ask and he knew it. Damien felt like he didn't deserve it.

Chapter 16

Time to Tell

Whilst James had been away, sorting out his old home and life, Simona had been organising their celebratory evening. The plan was for her to wear a rather special, easy-to-remove dress and as James arrived, she would offer him some champagne. Expecting that he would want to shower, Simona imagined that whilst he was doing so, Eliza could serve the delicious meal she had been preparing all afternoon and then, much later, they would dance by candlelight and consummate their celebration and future together. Expecting him to walk through the door at any moment, Simona was slightly startled when her mobile phone rang and it was James calling her.

Supposing he must be on his way home, Simona picked up her phone and swiped to accept the call. Feeling in a playful mood, she almost purred as she spoke, "Hello my darling, are you checking up on me? I am ready and waiting, you know."

Simona subconsciously rubbed her hand across her pregnant belly as she waited for his response. But Damien sounded distant, worried; he was about to disappoint her and that bothered him. "Simona, my darling, there's been an emergency here and I've had to take someone to hospital." Thinking how that sounded so lame and might raise more questions, he quickly added, "It's one of my neighbours, a friend and she's pregnant..." Damien stumbled over the words, digging his hole deeper and deeper with every lie. "They think she may have lost her baby."

As those words crossed his lips, his voice cracked and he struggled to control his emotions; he must try harder to ensure Simona didn't suspect anything, other than the story he was relaying.

Simona could hear the distress in James' voice and questioned which hospital he was in. Now feeling concerned for James' neighbour – a woman so obviously in need – Simona also felt doubly proud of her man, for rushing to help a true damsel in distress. Damien wasn't expecting Simona's question and answered without thinking, "We're at St. Bart's and it looks like she really has lost her baby." Damien was aware he was repeating himself, but the shock had affected him more than he realised. In that moment, he accidentally compromised not only his cover, but Inga's safety.

Feeling some sympathy – which was a reaction of her own pregnancy hormones – Simona wanted to help James in some way and offered to come and sit with him. Realising his unwitting disclosure could open up a hornets' nest if Simona showed up, Damien thanked her for her concern and hurriedly advised that there was no need. Reassuring her that it was most likely, he would be on his way back by the time she got there anyway, or soon after. Suggesting she wait for him at home, Damien advised that he would be back as soon as possible.

As Simona hung up the phone, she felt disappointment overwhelm her at the thought of the celebratory evening that she had planned so perfectly for them, which was obviously now completely trashed. Then, in an unexpected rush of admonished acceptance, she reminded herself of the woman James was helping. A woman who was not as lucky as she was, because she still had her baby. As Simona again rubbed her hand over her belly in a protective, yet comforting manner, she decided that maybe she would drive to that hospital and wait with James anyway. Simona wanted to feel useful and thought that at least they would be together, even if it was in a hospital waiting room and James would probably end up being glad she had gone, plus it meant he didn't have to rush back.

Pete had been trying to call Damien all day, but Damien had bounced his calls, until on the sixth attempt, when he finally answered, knowing that if anyone could possibly understand his dilemma, Pete might. Damien's voice sounded sad when he answered with his usual, "Hello mate," and, following the expected response from Pete, Damien explained what had happened to Inga. Naturally, leaving out the additional facts about Simona and the real reason for him resigning from the job he loved.

Pete was shocked and immediately insisted on driving over to sit with Damien, whilst they waited on news of Inga. Damien felt relieved and thanked Pete, explaining that he'd probably be in the maternity ward once they brought Inga out. It was a harsh fact that all baby-related admissions ended up in maternity, even if the baby was lost.

When Pete turned up an hour later, Kate was also with him. Damien groaned internally. There was no way he could now tell Pete what had happened in the run-up to him returning home and finding Inga unconscious. Understandably though, Kate wanted to be there for them both, she was worried sick and feeling desperately sad for both Damien and Inga. Saying as much, Kate was unable to imagine how awful it was to have lost their first and much longed-for child. The emotion was too much for them both as Kate rushed towards Damien, opening her arms to hug him tight on the news that they had actually lost twin girls. Damien knew Kate would never forgive him if she knew of his plans just a few hours ago, but he was grateful for the comfort her hug gave him. Damien needed and wanted to feel comforted, because he knew he had monumentally screwed up his life and now he had done the same to Inga's too.

As the three of them sat waiting, drinking the ghastly coffee that Kate had fetched from the drinks machine outside, they talked about what had happened when Damien got home and how Inga had looked when he first found her. It was like a gruesome post-mortem. Damien's detailed description of the scene was sobering to them all. Excusing himself from the discussion, Damien got up to find the toilets. As he stepped out into the corridor he glanced towards the Nurse Station, the duty nurse looked up and shook her head; no news as yet. Damien's shoulders sank a little lower as he made his way along the short corridor to the visitor's toilet and disappeared inside.

At that very same moment, Simona stepped out of the lift and walked along to the Nurse Station; she had found the address for the hospital and made her way to the maternity ward, having been told that anyone with pregnancy issues would have been taken there. Not knowing the patient's name, Simona was trying to explain who she was looking for, when Damien reappeared. Simona spotted him immediately and called out, "James, darling, I just couldn't sit and wait for you at home, what with you being so worried for your neighbour. So, I thought I'd drive down and sit with you here. It took no time at all because the roads were really clear. Mind you, it's miles from home!" Simona was babbling and beaming all at the same time, proud of herself for having played detective and found the exact place that James was waiting for his neighbour. The poor woman.

This was definitely a new Simona; she had changed and was behaving like someone who cared and felt compassion for others. It must be the hormones. Even Damien realised that and yet, as he looked at Simona's beaming face, he was so happy to see her, despite knowing his world was about to fall apart. Which, as if on cue, it just might, as Kate and Pete walked out into the hallway at the very same moment. Pete instantly recognised Simona and guessed this was a disaster waiting to happen, having also spotted her very pregnant belly. But, it was Kate who managed to speak first, exclaiming, "My goodness, what's Lowry's friend doing here?" Kate's eyebrows gave away her equally surprised shock on seeing the now obviously pregnant Simona, who had turned around on hearing Lowry's name.

"Kate?" Simona remembered Kate from Lowry's group of friends, and Pete. Although she couldn't quite remember his name, just his face.

"Oh, my goodness, what a coincidence," Simona beamed at Kate. "So, what are you guys doing here?"

Kate was struggling to make sense of the coincidence. "Hello again, it's Simona, isn't it? I was just going to say the same thing, but then I guess you're here because of your baby." Kate's statement stabbed a knife into Damien's gut.

"Kate, Simona, oh, of course, the BBQ." Damien was playing for time, trying to think of an explanation as Simona walked over to him and took his hand.

Kate stared, first at their clasped hands and then Damien's face as she begged the question, "Well, I can see we're obviously interrupting something here, so what's going on? Damien? Where is Inga?"

"Damien? Who's Damien?" Simona was puzzled. "James, what is this? How do you know Kate and..." Simona gestured towards Pete, "Damien?"

Damien blanched and stepped back against the wall, "Oh, Jesus, I didn't expect this to happen." As he looked from Simona to Kate and then to Pete, he wanted the ground to open up and swallow him. Instead, the expected and surprised question was asked simultaneously by both Kate and Simona.

"You didn't expect *what* to happen?" Kate's voice rose in pitch and tone as disbelief and the obvious conclusion took over her thoughts. Simona was obviously *with* Damien and presumably, by her reaction, she must be carrying his baby, but how? When? They'd only met Simona at the garden party. *Poor Inga.*

Kate's mind was racing, still trying to piece together this complicated puzzle, when Simona spoke again. "James, how do you know Kate and Damien?" Simona glanced at Pete, she certainly did recognise him, but hadn't remembered his real name.

Pete stepped in, immediately suspecting that Simona was why Damien's last undercover role had led to him resigning without warning. Clearly, Damien and Simona had become more than just MI5 spy and daughter of the now deceased Mafia Don that Damien had been investigating. Pete took Kate's arm and suggested that maybe they should go and get a coffee, just as Simona demanded that James explain everything and in an octave higher, added, "Right now!"

The nurse from along the corridor appeared beside the group and hushed them, saying to either lower their voices and return to the relative's room, or, leave immediately. The intervention stopped Simona in her tracks as the nurse also advised Damien that his wife was now in recovery and although weak, was doing well.

"Wife? What do you mean, wife?" Simona shrilled, her face aghast as she turned to James, demanding he explain what the nurse meant. Damien braced himself for the painful confession that was now required.

Kate watched in disbelief and shock, as Damien's world caved-in. The time had arrived and all he could do was to admit that yes, he had a wife and that no, the woman he had told her about wasn't his neighbour, she was his wife and it was *their* babies she has lost.

"WIFE? BABY?" Simona screeched at James, unable to believe what he'd just said. "You never said you had a WIFE, let alone that she was pregnant! How could you, James? I loved you!" Simona was reeling in shock, her hand pressed against her tummy, protecting her own baby, as she lunged forward and punched Damien in the face, hard. The nurse called for security. Kate turned to Pete and shaking her head, asked him what was going on. Of course, Pete had to deny knowing anything, but told Kate to wait in the visitors' room, while he sorted things out. As he turned towards Damien, Kate just stepped back, unable to leave the scene unfolding in front of her, but, before Pete could reach them, Simona had struck Damien again, this time with such force that he fell backwards, hitting his head on the corner of the doorframe with a dull thud that could only mean a bad outcome and as he hit the floor, the light left his eyes. A pool of blood began to form on the floor around Damien's head, as Simona, now distraught and shocked, held her hand to her mouth before turning tail and running towards the elevator, to furiously punch the call-button. Simona glanced back to watch the nurses, as well as Kate and Pete all trying to help her James.

As they fought to stem the bleed and resuscitate Damien, the elevator doors opened and the now crying Simona rushed inside, desperate to distance herself from the pain and damage she had just inflicted on James. Feeling scared, Simona wondered if she had just killed the man she loved and who was the father of her unborn baby. Not knowing where to go, Simona got out of the elevator on the next floor and wandered along the corridor until she found a room to hide in. She needed to think, needed to decide what to do. Then, realising she also needed to know what had happened to James, she left the safety of the room she had found and wandered until she found the stairwell, thinking she might be able to sneak upstairs and crack the door open, to listen to what was going on along the corridor. As she pushed open the stairwell door, she could hear an urgent voice. Pete had stepped into the stairwell too and was just above her. Simona clung to the wall and held her breath, hearing Pete reporting an internal code red and that Damien was involved.

As she listened to the coded speak, Simona realised Pete was obviously a cop, or something like that, and her James was obviously not the James she had known, and still loved. Neither was Pete this 'Damien' person! It was clear to her now, that James was really Damien, which meant her James was also a cop, or like Pete, something similar. Why else would he have changed his name?

Simona's heart was breaking at such a betrayal of both her and her father. How could James have fooled them all so well?

Pete now mentioned her name and said he'd let her go, knowing they could pick her up anytime, if necessary. Their first priority was to ensure Damien was okay and that Inga did not find out about Simona, until Damien could talk to her himself.

Simona was seething, shocked and scared. If she had killed James, or Damien, or whatever the heck his name was, she would be locked up and that wasn't an ending she relished. Not only that, she had lost her lover and the father of her baby. Simona held back the sobs until she heard Pete go back through the doors and then she fell to the floor, wrapping her arms around herself as she cried.

Damien was still unconscious and his head wound was bleeding profusely, despite the pressure-pad being held against it. The nurse was worried about him and extremely unimpressed. As if she didn't have enough to do with all her other patients, now she had to deal with a visitor incident and a serious one to boot. Security arrived via the elevator, apologising for the delay, explaining that there had been an incident in A&E which had taken priority. All was calm now though, so they were here to help.

"It seems to be a night of unexpected incidents." Pete tried to normalise the situation, knowing it was an impossible task. Mike was on his way and Pete had been ordered to stay with Damien. Not that he had any intention of leaving, besides, Kate needed him too. Confused and still not fully understanding what the hell was going on, Kate watched as the nursing staff worked on Damien. Having moved to stand with Pete, one thing Kate was certain of was that Inga would need her now, more than ever.

Wondering when Inga would be brought up to the ward, Kate waited patiently to ask the obvious questions as to where she would be put and where Damien would be taken to. Half an hour later, her question was answered as both Damien and Inga were moved to separate wards. Damien's being on the floor below, whilst Inga, because of the loss of her babies, would be moved to a side room of the maternity suite, so that she would at least have some privacy, away from the new mothers happily cradling their healthy babies.

Despite the generous gesture, Kate knew the cries of birthing mothers and new babies would still punish Inga's ears and break her heart every time she heard them, but at least in a private room, she couldn't see the mothers, or their babies. Entering Inga's room and seeing her friend lying there, pale and unconscious, with drips and all kinds of medical paraphernalia rigged up to monitor her progress following surgery, Kate grew even more angry with Damien. It was obvious to her, at least it seemed the only explanation, that Damien had been cheating on Inga and not only impregnated his wife, but he had gotten Simona pregnant too. Yet, even that explanation also made no sense because Kate knew that Lowry and Simona had been 'together' as a couple, so how did Damien fit in with that? Besides which, he'd had to dash off to work on the day of the BBQ, so how had they even met? Kate was confused. Simona must be bisexual, it was the only explanation Kate could think of, but it still left loose ends as to the how, when and where she and Damien had met. The ticker-tape thought process was running on overdrive in Kate's head as she tried to make sense of it all. Clearly, Simona was pregnant and she had been talking to Damien as if he was her boyfriend, but then, who was James? Kate flopped into the chair beside Inga's bed, now exhausted by the confused thoughts rushing through her brain. As she took Inga's hand in hers, Kate focussed on her friend and only hoped that Inga would pull through this and that losing her babies would not cause her to do anything stupid. What a terrible situation she would be waking up to!

A few minutes later, Pete came into the room, saying he would have to leave Kate on her own for now, but asking if she wanted him to call Shelley, or Emily. Kate shook her head. "No thanks Pete, I'll just wait here for Inga, we don't need any more confusion tonight. Let's just us sort things out first and then let the others know what's going on once we have more information."

"Okay, babe, well, I'll have to go back and stay with Damien until my relief arrives, so I'll see you back home after all this, although it could well be *very* late." Pete had no idea what Mike would do now, or if he himself would be asked to go back to Thames House to debrief tonight. As he hugged Kate, Pete told her he loved her and then was gone, back to his duties and helping Mike to sort out this terrible mess.

Not long after Pete had returned to Damien's room, Inga began to awaken, but, still feeling very sleepy from the anaesthetic and weak from both the blood loss and emergency surgery, she barely opened her eyes before closing them again, not wanting to wake up. Kate leant forward in the chair beside Inga's bed and whispered, "Hello honey, it's Kate, I'm here, don't you worry now, just sleep my darling girl." Kate continued to hold Inga's hand, gently stroking her fingers, trying to reassure her that everything was going to be alright. *Only it wasn't, was it, in fact, everything was far from being bloody all right!* The thoughts consumed Kate's mind as she watched her sleeping friend and finally allowed her own tears of sadness to fall. *How could this have happened? Damien and Inga had wanted this baby for so long and they seemed to love each other very much, despite their recent troubles and now he'd obviously gone off and had an affair! Not only that, he'd got the other woman pregnant too! It was just not fair!*

Several hours later...

"Damien?" Inga's voice was weak as she whispered her husband's name and slowly opened her eyes to see that it wasn't her husband holding her hand. Inga could just make out Kate's hair through the haze that was clouding her eyes. On hearing Inga speak, Kate lifted her head off the bed, having fallen asleep leaning against it a couple of hours ago. The nursing staff had worked around her, as they'd checked on Inga every fifteen minutes and hadn't minded, feeling thankful that Inga would have a friend with her when she woke up. It was going to be tough news for the poor woman to hear.

Kate smiled at Inga, relieved that her friend was awake and strong enough to speak, if only to whisper. The trouble was, she also knew that she now had to explain why Damien wasn't there. There had been no change in his condition, so all Kate could tell Inga was that it had been Damien who had found her and brought her into hospital. Not wanting to worry Inga, but knowing there was no escaping the truth, Kate carefully explained that Damien had somehow fallen backwards and hit his head on a doorframe and because the wound had bled a lot, he had been taken to another ward. Kate felt awful for not disclosing the full truth, but then, she didn't really know what that truth was and thought it best to drip-feed any information she did know, until Inga was stronger.

As Inga began to panic at the news that Damien was hurt, Kate quickly added that she was not to worry, he would be fine and it was all just a precaution because of the bleeding. Kate thought it really was best not to mention Simona, not until she knew more of what that story really was. But, what she had told Inga was at least true. Inga's memory of the previous day began slowly filtering through the numbness that was filling her mind, "My baby?" Kate sighed heavily, the weight of the news she had to share was too awful to speak out, but she had to. Inga needed to know and she was her friend.

"Oh, Inga, you lost so much blood... there was a tear in the uterus and... oh, my darling, you were carrying two girls." Her own tears welled over as Kate broke the worst possible news. "They said that both of your babies were

172

just too small to survive such a trauma. Oh, Inga, my darling, you have lost both your babies. I am so, very, very sorry. I wish this was..." Kate's sentence faded as she squeezed her friend's hand, not knowing what else to say, helplessly watching the terrible news she had just delivered register in Inga's mind and be immediately followed by complete anguish and utter disbelief. Kate's own sorrow was now uncontrollable, as she watched Inga's heart break, knowing her precious babies were no longer inside her – their hope for the future, their darling babies were gone, lost, to both her and Damien – and as the sobs racked Inga's limp body, Kate just held her friend as close as she could, wishing she could take away some of the pain, whilst knowing there was still more to come. Inga's grief totally overwhelmed her as Kate's arms held her tighter still. There was so much more to tell, once they all knew exactly what Damien's story was, but this was enough for now. Fearing Inga would not be able to cope with the news of her husband's infidelity, Kate comforted her friend as best she could, not knowing what else to do or say.

The nursing staff were used to this type of reaction from bereaved mothers and offered condolences and sympathy, but their words felt lame and didn't help. How could anything they said feel like help to Inga, it wasn't their babies that had been lost!

Down on the second floor, Damien's head injury was worse than they first thought and he was still unconscious. Mike had arrived and was talking to Pete outside the room. Pete was filling him in as best he could, with what limited information he knew. Mike cursed, he was angry about the fact that Damien had screwed up so badly and yet, he also felt frustrated that his now ex-colleague and friend, was lying unconscious and at serious risk of actually dying. Technically, whilst Damien was no longer Mike's official responsibility, because of Simona's involvement and the fact that she now knew Damien wasn't her 'James', that situation complicated matters and it was Mike who would have to deal with it. How he did that was the six-million-dollar question. Mike knew of other agents who'd gone rogue and how they had been dealt with, but he didn't want that for Damien, he felt he owed him that much for all the past good he had done.

Privately, Mike surmised how foolish Damien had been to let his sexual urges rule his head, but, Mike also knew that both he and the upper chain of MI5 command were just as much to blame, for exposing Damien to Simona and recommending he get 'as close to her as possible'. What the fuck did they think could happen? Sometimes, the decisions Mike was asked to force upon his team, made him question his own involvement and this was one of those moments. Knowing time was of the essence and that they had to get to Simona and find out how she was, Mike knew it was time to bring back Lowry; she was their only hope. Whilst he knew the risks were just as high, Mike accepted that Lowry could be regarded as collateral damage, should this situation blow-up even further. Not only that, he would now have to bring Pete further into the fray, his discreet handling of the situation so far, was admirable and without question. Mike had wanted Pete on his team and now his wish was being granted as he explained the background of Damien's last undercover role, what he'd achieved by working so closely with the Don and just how large a haul of drugs they had managed to seize and keep off the streets. By the time Mike had briefed Pete, a new sense of admiration for Damien had filled Pete's mind. Yes, the guy had fallen foul along the way, but wow, what a massive difference his undercover work had made and how many young lives he had potentially saved.

Pete felt for Damien, almost as much as Mike did. What a crazy situation this was and a completely impossible predicament that Damien had found himself in. Of course, neither man was aware that Simona had drugged Damien all those times they'd had sex. Nor were they aware of the fact that, had he not been drugged, his resistance to Simona would have been stronger and he may well have been able to resist her charms. Certainly, his role would have taken a different path and they probably would not have ended up here now, with Damien's life on the line. Mike refrained from sharing his current plan of involvement of Lowry, it was best that Pete didn't know anything more at this stage. Maybe later though.

As Mike left, he asked Pete to watch over Damien and update him as soon as there was any change, good or bad. Pete preferred to hope for the good and confirmed that he was okay to stay through the night, if necessary.

Chapter 17

Confused Minds

When Mike left the floor by the elevator, he did not see Simona sat out in the stairwell. With so little night-time movement of staff or visitors, nobody else had seen her there either. Not knowing what to do next and fearful of what she had already done to James, Simona had lost track of her senses and whilst Mike had been with Pete and Damien, she had taken herself off to a cloakroom and risked the life of her baby to take a line of cocaine.

Being a familiar user and in shock, Simona had not considered what even a small amount of cocaine could do to her, whilst in a state of pregnancy hormonal changes. Thinking it would help to calm the pain and ease her tormented mind, Simona was taken by surprise at how strong the drug was, even for someone used to taking it. With her being pregnant, the results were never going to be good, but again, Simona didn't even think of that and as the drug took hold of her mind, pumping its poison around her brain, she soon became demented, tortured by what should have been the happiest of times. Ever since losing her father and thinking she had also lost James, Simona had felt a deep and extreme sadness, so, to then have James back in her life again, had been nothing short of a miracle to her. Their reunion had filled Simona with so much joy and happiness. Now though, her worries and fears were in control and Simona could not bear the thought of losing James again, no matter what he had done.

Pulling herself up using the handrail, Simona leaned heavily against the wall. Feeling sad and uncomfortable, she steadied her balance and took a step forward; her plan was to find the room James was in, so she could tell him she was sorry and that it didn't matter about his wife, because she knew he loved her, he'd told her so, hadn't he? Which meant they could put all of this behind them. After all, there was no other baby now anyway, so he could come home with her and they could live together with their own baby and all would be well. Spurred on by the drugs she had taken, Simona's thinking and belief was strong, so without a doubt in her mind that all would be well, she walked slowly along the corridor, looking for James' room.

Seeing Pete coming out of James' room, Simona hesitated before very quickly slipping into another room, so he wouldn't see her. Pete had seemed like a nice guy at the party, but she knew from what he'd said earlier, that he was obviously a cop – Code Red, he'd said – she remembered that much despite the drug-induced state of her mind. The patient whose room she had entered, stirred in their sleep, "Shush!" Simona tried to quieten them, worried about being found, but the patient was already fast asleep and wasn't even aware she was there.

Watching through the slightly open door, Simona saw Pete walk towards the toilet, so, taking advantage of the opportunity, she hurried along the corridor and into James' room. Immediately taking his hand in hers and gently kissing his face, Simona begged and pleaded with him to forgive her earlier reaction. Telling him that it really didn't matter about his wife and just repeating to him all of the things she had thought about, out on the stairs.

Damien was unconscious, but he was aware of Simona's voice; she was close by, somewhere, but just out of his reach, he could hear her talking to him, but he couldn't respond.

James' face smiled and Simona knew he had heard her, she was so happy and as she told him she loved him, at that very same moment, Pete returned. Simona panicked and assumed that Pete would want to arrest her or something, so she grabbed hold of the drip tube that was attached to James' arm and threatened to pull it out. Pete tried to calm her down, but the cocaine was coursing through her veins and sending her crazy. Simona knew she had to get out, she had to get away, past Pete, but he was blocking the doorway. Pete's hands were held up, palms facing her, trying to calm her down.

Damien could hear the commotion, but he couldn't quite wake up, all he could see in his mind's eye, was a vision of his broken Inga, but he could hear Simona, she was ranting, what was going on with her?

Just at that moment, Damien groaned and as Pete looked towards him, Simona made a break for it, but as she did so, Pete grabbed her, telling her not to be scared, whilst noticing that her pupils were completely dilated and with her being pregnant, he immediately let her go. Panicking even more, Simona ran down the corridor and hurried back up the stairs, holding her tummy to prevent it bouncing her baby around. Pete called the nurses and rushed after Simona with them, but she was already out of sight and as they all rushed down the stairs, thinking she was making for the exit, Simona made it up the stairs, to the floor that Inga was on.

Once again, Simona approached the Nurse Station, but there was nobody there and so she took the opportunity to look for Inga's room. It couldn't be too hard, each room had the patient's name on the door and even though she didn't know Inga's last name, because she had heard them refer to 'Inga' earlier, she assumed there would likely be only one Inga on the ward.

As Simona entered Inga's side-room, she could see the light was dimmed. Inga was sleeping again, exhausted by her earlier tears and the remainder of the anaesthetic. Kate was nowhere to be seen, having first gone to the bathroom and then fetching herself a drink from the relative's room. Staring down at her rival in love, Simona's own emotions overwhelmed her, mixing pity for the loss of Inga's babies, with jealousy at this woman already being James' wife. Not only that, until today, she had been his *pregnant* wife and being James' wife was something Simona had thought of herself becoming. She had wanted to be the first, his one and only. It was something she still truly wanted. But, as the combination of her pregnancy hormones and the cocaine took over, any sense of clarity in her mind was now fogged and confused. Simona began to feel anger towards both Inga and James. How dare he get her pregnant when his so-called *wife* was also pregnant! Simona wanted revenge for the hurt and disappointment flooding her mind and senses; she needed to end the pain that was wracking her emotions. As she reached for the drip-tube feeding Inga's arm, she thought of tugging it out, but instead, she took the drip-bag down and threw it to the floor, stopping the lifesaving fluid from entering Inga's bloodstream. Unable to quite bring herself to do anything more than that – she was not her father after all – Simona spoke aloud, hoping Inga would somehow hear her words.

"It is *I* who loves James, he is no longer your husband because *I* am having his baby and I will have **him** too!"

With that, Simona turned on her heel and rushed out of the door, making her way to the elevator. She escaped without notice and again returned to James' floor, hoping that Pete would be gone by now. But, as she reached the room, she could see through the glass panel that Pete was sat beside James and so she gave up her attempts to see him again and turned to leave. She didn't feel well now and needed to sit down where nobody could see her. Thinking of the safety of her car, Simona made her way outside into the cool evening air. Remembering how happy she had been as she'd driven down to surprise James and sit with him, as any loyal girlfriend would, Simona began to cry. Reaching her car, she sank heavily into the driver's seat and laid her head on her arms, across the steering wheel. With despair filling her heart, Simona sobbed, for James, who it seems, wasn't James, and for the loss of her dream of a future with him. How could they recover from this, where would it all end? Would James be okay, or had she accidentally killed him? Simona was exhausted and in a heightened emotional state, but, she also wanted to go home and so she started the car and without thinking about her seatbelt, made her way out of the hospital grounds.

There was no way that Simona should have even attempted to drive, but any shred of common sense she might previously have had, was gone and all that remained was the effects of the drugs she'd taken earlier. Not realising that she was driving erratically with her foot pressing down hard on the accelerator, Simona began to speed along the roads that took her from the hospital to the motorway and which would eventually get her home. Managing not to crash her car on the motorway, Simona pulled off the brightly lit road onto the narrow country lanes which ultimately led to her family home. Now feeling a little light-headed because she had not eaten or drunk anything for hours and knowing her blood sugar levels were low, Simona felt shaky and realised she should stop, but, knowing the food and fluids she needed awaited her at home, she ignored that realisation and carried on. Pushing her foot down harder, the car veered to the wrong side of the road as she approached the bend too fast. Simona slammed her foot on the brakes to better negotiate the bend, causing her car to lose traction and spin around, completing a one-hundred and eighty degree turn before heading towards the hedge, just as a large truck rounded the bend and crashed into the side of her car. The impact carried Simona's car twenty-feet down the lane and with no seatbelt to hold her, she was thrown from side to side, her head smashing into the side window as the crumpling car took the full impact of the collision.

When the two vehicles finally ground to a halt, the truck driver, who was shocked but unhurt, climbed down from his wrecked cab to help the woman in the car he'd just smashed into. *Please God, let her be okay*. The poor man was beside himself with worry, as he pulled his phone from his pocket to make the emergency call for police, ambulance and fire brigade. It was clear they would need to cut her out and as he looked inside the car, he cried out, *"Oh, my God, she's pregnant!"* The poor truck driver began to panic; his own daughter was pregnant too and all he could imagine was this young woman being his own little girl. Trying to awaken the unconscious Simona, the truck driver couldn't get her out of the car, her legs were trapped and she was too badly injured for him to move her anyway. Instead, he followed the paramedic's advice on the phone and supported her head, ensuring her airway was clear. The ambulance would be ten to fifteen minutes they said.

The truck driver's name was Ben and as he introduced himself to Simona, even though she was unconscious. It made him feel better to speak to her, because that way, it felt like she was going to be okay. Simona was drifting, unable to feel pain, she could hear a voice comforting her and telling her everything would be okay. It sounded like her father's voice, but she knew it wasn't him. The voice was calling her 'sweetheart' and reassuring her that they would be here soon to cut her out, and that she and her baby would be fine. Of course, she didn't know what he meant, or who 'they' were, but Simona knew that she and her baby were still together, still connected, still one.

Inside her heart, Simona knew they were going to be fine because she could feel a warmth comforting her and on seeing a bright, loving light, she just knew they were saved. All she had to do was walk towards the light. If only her legs would work, but they felt heavy and useless. Simona cried out to her father to help her and in that moment, he appeared, smiling and healthy, with no signs of the gunshot wound which had taken his life. Simona was ecstatic and reached out her arms; her Daddy was here, he would help them both, her and her baby. As her father reached out to her, the loving light surrounded them, accepting them as it lifted both mother and baby away from the heaviness of trapped legs and crushed metal and transporting them to a happier place, one filled with love, light and her beloved father. Never again to experience pain in this lifetime, Simona's father reassured her that yes, they would be taking her baby girl with them.

As Simona walked with her father and baby daughter, he spoke of the grave mistakes he had made and which he now very much regretted; also mentioning the tough life she had experienced after losing her own mother whilst still so young. Simona's soul was still young and inexperienced in the ways of the greater being and so, he explained, they would need to return again, another time, to learn the lessons they had each missed in this life. But, he reassured her, it was fine, because it was expected.

Simona was happy to leave this life because she was with her father and her baby and she felt glad about that, and whilst knowing she would be coming back another time, that was also fine with her, because there was still something she needed to prove to herself, she just didn't quite know what that was, just yet.

Chapter 18

Who Knows What the Future Holds

With the drip-bag having been discovered fallen from the stand, soon after Simona had left and following the quick reactions of her medical team, Inga was saved from further harm. The expectation was that there would be no long-term effects caused by this hiccup. Although, the registrar did advise the nursing team that Inga would likely continue to feel groggy for a few more days.

Unaware of the drama cause by Simona's return and having gone outside to drink her coffee and get some air whilst her friend slept, Kate now walked back into Inga's room. On seeing several nurses and the registrar surrounding her friend, Kate panicked, begging to know what was going on and asking if Inga was okay? Having been told of the reason for the flurry of activity, Kate mused as to whether Simona had somehow found Inga and been tampering with the equipment, or if a nurse had just not fixed the bag properly. Deciding she was being crazy and that it was just a bag not being hung properly, rather than anything more sinister, Kate was relieved to hear that Inga was going to be okay and that no real harm had been done. However, despite reassuring Kate, the registrar was puzzled; it was extremely unusual for this to happen. More than that though, he was also very concerned that Inga may want to pursue a legal complaint as to where the fault lay. Thankfully though, all seemed to be well and Inga was responding, so there was no recompense to worry over.

Despite her grief over the loss of their baby girls, Inga's will to live was strong and she knew she had to pull through, because Damien needed her. Of that she was certain, particularly now, knowing he had hurt his head quite badly following the fall, which she knew must be bad, otherwise he would be here with her. Still the loyal and devoted wife, Inga was also still unaware of the dreadful deceit that Damien had managed to inflict upon their marriage.

The registrar and nursing staff left the room, having reassured Inga that whilst she was still very weak, the temporary lack of viscosity fluids was a small setback and unlikely to extend the period of time they expected it would take, before she would be strong enough to go home.

Now alone together in the room, Inga asked Kate to find out how Damien was doing and ask his medical team if she could see him. Eyeing-up the drips and wires Inga herself was still hooked up to, Kate said it was doubtful that Inga would be allowed out of bed, but that yes, of course she would go check on Damien and ask about taking Inga down to see him.

As Kate reached the floor that Damien's room was on, she paused and took a breath, a darkness was creeping over her and it felt as if there was only bad news ahead of her. Reaching Damien's room, Kate rushed into Pete's arms, needing his love and the comfortable safety of his embrace, then looking towards Damien, she exclaimed, "Oh, my God, Pete, he really doesn't look good, does he?" It was a statement of fact, rather than a question, but Kate was right, Damien was not good. The head injury had caused a major bleed inside his brain and despite the emergency surgery he'd had, the prognosis was uncertain. It would be a case of waiting, watching and hoping. The surgeon had told Pete that Damien stood a fifty-fifty chance of a full recovery. The alternative, if he even survived, was serious brain damage, but wanting his patient's visitor to remain positive, the surgeon chose to withhold the detailed description.

Pete explained to Kate exactly what the surgeon had said and suggested she go home and freshen up. Kate nodded and said she would just pop back up to Inga, to let her know Damien was being kept sedated whilst his brain recovered from the surgery. There seemed little point in Inga being brought down, but Kate knew that if the roles were reversed and it was Pete lying there, even if he was unconscious, she would want to sit with him. Relaying her thoughts to Pete, Kate was surprised when he agreed with her, not realising that Pete had been thinking exactly the same thoughts – had it been her, his beloved Kate, lying unconscious in that bed – so, they agreed that if the nursing staff said it was okay, Kate should bring Inga down, if that was at all possible.

However, their request was immediately overridden by Inga's own nursing team, who advised that she really should not get out of bed, due to her unstable blood pressure. It was too dangerous at this point and there wasn't a nurse available to go with them. Apologising, they also added that whilst today was not possible, maybe tomorrow – if Inga was more stable – she could go down. Whilst extremely disappointed, Inga was thankful of Kate's attempts and her update on Damien, even though it left her more worried than she had been before. In her distressed state of mind, Inga had not realised quite how serious Damien's injury was, having also not been aware of the emergency surgery he had undergone. After more tears and hugs with Kate, Inga suggested Kate go home to eat and rest properly, adding that she herself needed some time alone anyway.

Kate agreed and said she would be back later with Pete and some fresh clothes and toiletries, for Inga to use. Thankful for such a good friend, Inga raised her hand in a weak wave as Kate left to go back downstairs to Pete.

Damien's thoughts were active inside his head despite his brain injury and he imagined he could see two women, Simona and Inga, each holding babies and each of them angry with him for the hurt he had caused. Then Inga's face seemed to distort and the vision of her and their baby crumpled, leaving behind an invading sense of devastation. Damien could make no sense of the random thoughts cascading throughout his mind and yet, somehow, he also knew he'd done something very wrong, but he could not quite remember what it was. Who was Simona and why was she in his mind and whose baby was she holding? There was a bright light surrounding them, which was both beautiful and comforting. Damien could feel himself being drawn towards the light as Simona held out the baby girl for him to take from her, but he didn't understand why. Damn, whose baby was it and why was she calling him James?

With no recollection of his recent life with Simona, the damage to Damien's brain was such that it had wiped much of his short-term memory. Where was Inga? He needed Inga. Why wasn't she with him? The thoughts were driving him crazy. Where was he anyway? The bed felt strange, not like his own bed. Where was Inga?

BANG! There was an explosion in his head and everything went black. Pete jumped up as Damien flat-lined. Doctors and nurses rushed into the room and Pete found himself pushed towards the window, watching the crazy scene unfolding in front of him as they tried to revive Damien.

Kate reappeared at the door, shocked to see the drama In front of her, she stood frozen to the spot, her hand automatically covered her mouth stifling a cry of sadness at the realisation that Damien had crashed. Watching helplessly, as the medical teams repeated attempts to restart his heart, which failed again and again. The team continued working on Damien for a good fifteen minutes, but it was no use, his pupils were blown and unresponsive, and his heart was no longer beating. Damien had died.

Kate and Pete were in shock. They had known the bleed was bad, but somehow, neither thought he would die. As the doctor in charge called time of death, Kate's knees crumpled and Pete rushed towards her. Both of them horrified and already wondering how the hell Inga was going to cope with losing their babies and now her husband too. Kate was sure that Inga would not be able to take the shock of such devastating news.

The couple held onto each other, as the staff turned to them, apologising for Pete and Kate's loss as they each left the room, leaving one remaining nurse, who unplugged everything, gently commenting that Pete and Kate could stay with Damien for as long as they needed. Both of them knew that Inga would want to see Damien and asked if that would now be possible. They even offered to wheel her bed and her drip-stand down themselves. If that was allowed? The nurse said to leave it with her and that she would go and find out.

Having spoken with the ward staff upstairs, the nurse returned ten minutes later, with a trolley saying she had spoken to the staff nurse on Inga's ward and that they had agreed to transfer her to the trolley and wheel Inga down. The circumstances were exceptional and they too wondered how their already bereft patient would now cope with losing her husband too.

Kate left with the nurse to fetch Inga. Pete took that moment to call Mike, before saying his own goodbyes to

Damien. Pete was in shock, this could not be real. Yet, he knew that it was only too real and that their lives would never be the same, not for any of them, ever again.

As Mike took the news about Damien, he advised Pete that the team who had been listening in at Simona's house had also heard the call which Eliza had taken. It was the police, calling the number listed as 'home' on Simona's mobile, to advise that she had been involved in a road traffic accident and that with regret, they were calling to advise that neither Simona, nor her baby had survived. Eliza had screamed in pain down the telephone, causing Armand to come rushing into the room. Having dropped the telephone receiver, Eliza had slumped to the floor. Armand wrapped his arms around her and lifted her up while asking what had happened. Devastation overtook them as they realised that the family they had looked after for so long, were now gone. Both wiped out within weeks of one another. Was it karma paying a visit for all the wrongdoings of Simona's father and Simona's own recent silliness? Eliza and Armand would never know, because they were unaware of the many killings the Don had been involved with. What they would come to find out though, was that the family home they had looked after so lovingly was to become their own home, left to them by the Don, should Simona not survive long enough to have her own family. A thought which had grieved the old man when his will had been rewritten and that line added by his lawyer. The Don had, of course, hoped that Simona would live a long and eventful life, filling their home with little ones. But, sadly, fate had taken a hand and changed those plans in the most unexpected way.

It was too much for Pete, who was reeling as Mike tried to get his own head around the disaster that was now lying with him. Hearing about Simona was such a shock, but now Damien was gone too and whilst Mike was devastated at that news, experience taught him that he had to pull himself together and quickly. Saying to Pete that he would call him back later, Mike hung up.

Needing time to compose himself, it was fifteen minutes before Mike called an emergency team meeting to advise everyone of what had happened.

Inga could not believe what was happening, why was Kate telling her that Damien was now dead, when he was fine just half an hour ago? Yes, he was recovering from emergency surgery, but he was expected to pull through. At least, Inga had expected and assumed he would. Not knowing that she had been alone in that optimism. Everyone else had been feeling wary, knowing how delicate these cases could be. All of them had hoped Damien would be strong enough to pull through, whilst also expecting that the worst outcome could happen at any moment. It had been a fifty-fifty chance after all.

Damien was gone, her precious Damien, the man she loved and who she had hoped to grow old with, just gone, in the blink of an eye. Inga's heart broke and her emotions overtook her body, as, hanging on to Kate, she cried as if she would never stop. The nurse left them alone and said to call her when Inga was ready to be taken downstairs. Kate nodded as her own tears fell into Inga's hair, both women drowning in grief for Damien and the two babies that Inga had lost.

Chapter 19

Secrets and Promises

The funerals for both Damien and their baby girls were to take place three weeks after that awful day. Inga, supported by Kate and Pete, was a shadow of her former self. Grief and pain had taken over her life and it would be a long time before she could look to the future with any hope.

Although thankful for her very good friends, Kate and Pete, as well as Shelley and Emily, Inga felt pangs of envy whenever she saw any couples together, or babies being held by excited new mums. Life was painful enough for her and as they all now stood at the graveside and watched the two coffins being lowered into the earth, even Pete, who knew the truth, felt it was right and proper that their babies be buried together and in the same grave as Damien. For Inga's sake, Pete vowed to never share the truth he knew. There was no need now. Simona was gone and no-one needed to know about Damien's indiscretion, not as far as he was concerned.

Pete had forgotten about Lowry though and as he glanced towards her now, his heart sank, wondering if she already knew about Damien and Simona. Thankfully, it seemed that she did not and Pete breathed a small sigh of relief. Lowry had been protected from that truth, Mike had seen to it that Damien had been kept away from her and any discussions about Simona.

As Mike stood with his team, there to honour a man he had once called a friend, an emotion he was not used to feeling overwhelmed him and whilst struggling not to let it show, he watched as Inga bent down to pick up a handful of earth. As she threw it into the open grave of her small family and cried out her goodbyes, everyone gasped, their own pain for Inga was raw and empathetic. Tears fell as each person recognised her pain and felt thankful for their own blessings. Kate helped Inga to stand up again and comforted her friend as Inga's heartbreak overtook her whole being.

Like Pete, Kate had already decided never to reveal to Inga what she had surmised – having seen Simona with Damien at the hospital – but, in that small moment, she wavered for the briefest of times, before resolving again that Inga was to be protected. All that telling the truth would do, would be to break Inga's heart forever and Kate could not do that to her friend, so she contented herself with the knowledge that she was protecting Inga. Although it was a burden she was willing to bear and whilst appreciating that some things are best left unsaid, Kate also knew that damaging and vital piece of information would torment her forever. No thanks to Damien.

Pete wanted to know more and one day he hoped he would. This whole situation made him realise that more than ever before, this life he shared with Kate was precious to him beyond belief and no matter what happened at work, no way would he ever do to Kate what Damien had done to Inga. Even as he made that promise to himself, Pete was still totally unaware of the drugs Simona had used to influence Damien's behaviour and actions. Perhaps if drugs had never been introduced, Damien's life might have travelled a different path; one where he remained faithful to his beloved Inga. Pete decided if Damien *had* done that, he would probably still be here today, supporting his wife as they buried their babies. But that sad loss had long been predicted as their joint path in life and could never have been avoided.

Kate squeezed Pete's hand and knowing what she too was thinking, he glanced at her as, looking deep into her eyes he whispered quietly, "I love you, Kate."

About the Author

Having grown-up mainly in the South East of England, to live by the sea has always been a dream for Johanna and she is extremely grateful, after all the years of working and waiting, to now be living that dream and enjoying the stunning sea-views that Cornwall offers, along with the sense of calm that living by the sea brings to her life.

Johanna feels very lucky to have met a great number of quite different people throughout her life and those many different personalities, and shared life-stories, have created a well from which Johanna draws-on, to create her characters and storylines. Johanna describes it as picking snippets from her own and others real-life experiences, whilst leaving the rest to her creative imagination!

Answering a question about what life-advice she would give, Johanna told us, "Keep thinking about your dreams, no matter how impossible they may seem, because the magic of visualisation really does work. Your thoughts and intentions will become your reality, so be careful what you wish for! You don't need to worry about the route, just keep the destination in mind, work hard, keep believing and enjoy the ride!"

Other books by Johanna Jackson

Love Twists as Life Turns

In Casey's mind she is a twenty-something female, who is shocked to find she has reached her thirties whilst still unmarried. Feeling lucky to have good friends around her, Casey enjoys her single life and the attentions of more than one man. With a good dose of raunchy fun and the complications that multiple men can bring, Casey's life is certainly interesting. The involvement of these men in her life provides much anticipation and excitement, as well as several thought provoking situations for Casey to deal with.

It is Casey's experiences of friendship, loss, lust and worries, along with her dreams, which she decides to share in an *Online Diary*. In doing so, she captures the interest of someone who is able to influence great change in Casey's life, just at a point when a serious issue interrupts her progress.

Kellie's Dreams

Craving a calm, peaceful and uncomplicated life, through unexpected circumstances, Kellie finds herself living back in the same place she spent her childhood holidays.

As life begins to settle, strange dreams start to invade her senses and Kellie finds herself drawn back to ancient Egypt, the very subject she studied in university. An old love triangle re-surfaces, keeping Kellie guessing as to what it all means.

Sudden and unexpected events cause the life she has come to know to take a dramatic turn, but as time passes, previously untold stories emerge. The people in her life change again and Kellie finds herself facing a different connection; one which seems to link people from this life and a distant past.